Prescription: Romance™

"Tom, is this your daughter?"

Annie had to ask the question, and Tom couldn't deny that it was his baby.

"So…what will you do with her?"

"I haven't the faintest idea." Tom shook his head. "Annie! You have to look after her."

"You can't look after your own daughter?"

"You've done some pediatric training. I haven't done anything."

"Yes, you have, Tom," Annie said gently. "You've fathered a child. Welcome to fatherhood, Dr. McIver. Welcome to responsibility. Yours. Not mine."

Marion Lennox has had a variety of careers—medical receptionist, computer programmer and teacher. Married, with two young children, she now lives in rural Victoria, Australia. Her wish for an occupation that would allow her to remain at home with her children, her dog and the budgies led her to attempt writing a novel.

Prescription: Romance™

Dr. McIver's Baby
Marion Lennox

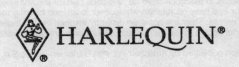

HARLEQUIN®

TORONTO • NEW YORK • LONDON
AMSTERDAM • PARIS • SYDNEY • HAMBURG
STOCKHOLM • ATHENS • TOKYO • MILAN • MADRID
PRAGUE • WARSAW • BUDAPEST • AUCKLAND

ISBN 0-373-83383-0

DR. McIVER'S BABY

First North American Publication 1998.

This edition published by arrangement with Harlequin Books S.A.

Printed in U.S.A.

CHAPTER ONE

DR ANNIE BURROWS seemed to spend her life avoiding Tom McIver's dogs and Tom McIver's women. Tripping over Tom's baby was the last straw.

The baby must have arrived just before midnight, but neither Annie nor Tom had heard it come.

Annie had sat up until twelve, doing medico-legal letters. Then she figured she'd have to sleep some time—and if she wanted any sleep she'd have to knock on Tom's door and tell him to keep the noise down.

There was sound-proofing between Tom's apartment and the hospital wards, but not between Tom's and Annie's apartments. A woman's laughter was making Annie wince, his stereo was playing too loud and one of his dogs was barking at the rising moon.

'Shut up, Hoof. Or Tiny. Whoever you are,' Annie muttered to Tom's out-of-sight dogs as she walked out into the darkened corridor.

And then her foot caught on something soft, and before she could recover Annie sprawled heavily over a bundle, lying in Tom's doorway.

Annie wasn't hurt. She was just plain furious.

For more than ten seconds Annie lay full length on the linoleum floor and swore. Swore at bachelor doctors who left their belongings strewn in the hallway. Swore at the woman who was still giggling inside. Swore at Tom's dogs who were both now barking hysterically on the other side of the door.

'I'll murder him! If this keeps up I'll commit real violence!'

Maybe she'd have to leave Bannockburn. She couldn't stand Tom McIver much longer.

The thought made her even angrier. Annie didn't

want to leave. Bannockburn was lovely. It was a tiny south Australian town, nestled in a coastal valley. The twelve-bed hospital needed two doctors to run it, and the doctors were Tom and Annie.

Tom McIver was a GP surgeon, a skilled clinician who concentrated one hundred per cent when he was working. He also concentrated one hundred per cent when he was playing—be it with his pair of huge Great Danes or his various women. It seemed to Annie that there wasn't a pretty face in the district Tom McIver hadn't been seen with. Tom's startling good looks had the valley girls smitten, and Tom made the most of it.

And Annie?

In her mid-twenties, Annie was seven years younger than Tom and had only been in Bannockburn for eight months. She studious and quiet—a GP with anaesthetic and paediatric skills. Tom had obstetric training so in tandem they worked brilliantly. It was only personally that Tom drove Annie nuts.

So Annie lay sprawled in the corridor and thought dark thoughts about her future—and even darker thoughts about Tom McIver. Then the bundle lying under Annie's legs moved.

Annie sat up as if she'd been burned. The package was alive! In one swift action she scooped the bundle into her arms. It was warm and moist and, as Annie lifted it, from the depths came a plaintive cry that told Annie this was no puppy or kitten.

This was a human child.

Tom's dogs had heard the sounds of Annie falling and the cry of the baby. The barking on the other side of Tom's door reached a crescendo.

The door burst open and a stream of light slashed down over her. Tom McIver stood in the doorway while his two damned dogs launched themselves at Annie, attempting to lick her to death. Somewhere behind him a woman was trying to peer round Tom's broad shoulders.

'Tom, what is it? Is it a prowler?'

'It's Annie,' Tom said blankly. 'Annie, why are you sitting on the floor?'

Annie didn't answer. With one hand she was fending off Tom's huge dogs, and with the other she was desperately trying to see what lay underneath the cloth. She'd fallen hard. Had she hurt it? She bent her body over the child in an effort to protect it, and then Tom was stooping beside her.

'Are you hurt? Annie, what is it. . .?'

And then he saw what she was holding.

'What the hell. . .?'

'Get the dogs off,' Annie snapped. 'Now.'

She'd hardly finished saying it before the dogs were gone. When Tom moved, he moved fast. Annie had never been able to fault Tom as a doctor, and in an emergency there was no one she would prefer to work with. Now, suddenly, the corridor light was on, Tom's dogs and his woman were behind his closed door and the baby on Annie's lap had all Tom's attention.

'What's wrong? Annie, what is going on here?'

'I don't know,' Annie muttered. She was peeling away layers of blanket. The child was dressed in a simple white towelling suit. Its tiny face was screwed up in anger and, as it started to cry, its legs and arms moved with an ease that told Annie there couldn't be major damage. The layers of woollen blanket had protected the child well.

'Everything seems OK,' Annie said, her hands running swiftly over the little body. 'I'll get it somewhere warm and undress it. . .'

'Annie. . .' Tom sat back on his heels and stared at Annie as though she'd lost her senses.

'Yes?' Annie flashed him a glance and then turned back to the baby.

Tom was looking decidedly dishevelled. His deep brown curls were tangled, he was wearing old jeans and a shirt which was undone to the waist—revealing far too much chest—and there was a trace of lipstick

on his collar. The sight of Tom's body had the power
to unsettle Annie. It always did. Now, as always, her
defence was to concentrate on her work.

'Annie, would you mind telling me just what the hell
is going on? Who is this?'

'I don't know,' Annie said simply. She undid a button
on the baby's towelling suit and took a peek under the
nappy. 'It's a girl.' She looked up at Tom and pressed
her lips together. 'Dr McIver, this baby was lying on
your doorstep. Does she belong to your friend in there?'

'You have to be kidding!' Tom smiled, with the mag-
netic laughter in his deep brown eyes that made him
an instant hit with each of his women in turn. And
unsettled Annie no end.

'Do you think we'd let the dogs in and leave a baby
outside?' Tom demanded of Annie, his ridiculous sense
of humour obviously caught. 'For heaven's sake. . .'
Then his smile faded. 'Where did you say the baby
was lying?'

'On your doorstep. I tripped over her.'

Tom's smile disappeared completely as he heard the
concern in Annie's voice. 'You tripped over her. . .'

'If she doesn't belong to your friend then she's been
dumped,' Annie said slowly. 'She's only about two
months old. She can hardly have crawled here by herself.' She looked down at the tiny bundle in her arms
and she felt her heart twist. The little girl was sobbing
her heart out. Who on earth would dump a child
like this?

She looked up and Tom's expression matched hers.
The laughter had faded completely as the seriousness
of what was happening hit home. Soundlessly, Tom
held out a hand and helped Annie to her feet. Annie
rose and let him steady her, and as she did a folded
piece of paper came loose from the child's wrappings
and fluttered to the floor.

Tom swooped and had it unfolded before Annie had
even straightened. She nestled the child into her arms,

crooning and rocking it until the child's distress eased. Then she looked back at Tom, and found his face had lost every vestige of colour.

'Tom?'

Tom didn't answer. He was staring at the paper as if he were staring at a nightmare.

'What is it?' Annie's voice was gently insistent, and it cut across Tom's shock. He lifted his face and stared at her—but he wasn't seeing Annie.

Which was nothing new. Annie was a diminutive five feet four inches tall. She kept her soft brown curls knotted severely back from her face. Her clear grey eyes were well hidden behind glasses, and her face showed more determination and honesty than loveliness. Compared to the willowy beauties Tom McIver favoured, Annie was plain, and the first time he'd seen her she'd known only a doctor who could reduce his workload. Nothing more.

Which she shouldn't mind at all, she told herself ten times a day. From childhood people had thought of Annie as plain, and they'd told her so. Bluntly.

She should be used to it.

And she shouldn't be thinking of it now when this little one was in such trouble.

'Tell me what the note says, Tom,' Annie asked again. She could have taken it from him. By the blank look on Tom's face she knew his fingers could hardly grasp a thing, but Annie's arms were full of baby.

Finally Tom pulled himself together, and focused on something other than the note.

'I'll show you. . .show you soon.' Tom took a ragged breath and visibly squared his shoulders. 'Annie, she'll have to be checked. You take her down to Children's Ward and examine her. I'll get rid of. . .I'll say goodnight to Sarah and be with you as soon as I can.'

'You're sure this isn't Sarah's baby?' Annie asked, and Tom stared at her blankly.

'No. No. . . Melissa. . .'

Tom put a hand up to his eyes and the impression of nightmare deepened. 'No,' he repeated. 'It's not Sarah's. Just. . . Just check her, will you, Annie? I'll be with you. . .I'll be with you when I can.'

Annie's paediatric skills weren't called for. Medically, the baby was just fine.

Bannockburn Hospital was quiet tonight, with four of its twelve beds empty. There was no one in the two-bed children's ward, but Helen, Bannockburn's more than capable night sister, bustled in soon after Annie arrived to see what she was doing. She stayed to help, and together they checked the baby completely. Annie didn't tell Helen what she was looking for and, apart from a couple of sideways looks at Annie, Helen didn't enquire.

The result? One healthy six-week-old baby girl. Well cared for. Great set of lungs. Just starting to smile, with a lopsided grin that went straight to the heart. Just starting to fuss about her next feed. Helen made up formula while Annie dressed the baby in dry hospital clothes. She cuddled the baby close, smiled down at that infectious grin and thought of what to do next.

'So, who is she?' Helen asked as she handed over a prepared bottle. Annie hadn't told her anything. She wanted to see Tom's note,before announcing publicly that the child had been dumped.

'Tom asked me to have a look at her,' Annie said ambiguously. She hitched herself up on the examination table, her denim-clad legs swinging. Then she took the warmed bottle from Helen and popped it into one eager little mouth. The baby's eyes widened in amazement— as though she hadn't expected anything as wondrous as a bottle—and she attacked the teat as if there were no tomorrow.

Annie looked down and found herself smiling into the baby's wide brown eyes. Some baby!

Helen gazed at Annie, her kindly eyes speculative.

In the few months Annie had been at Bannockburn Helen had taken Annie under her wing. The senior nurse had a kindness for the new young doctor—and she seemed to have a knack of knowing what Annie was thinking.

Helen's eyes said she knew there was something going on—something Annie knew and Helen didn't.

'Do we know her name?' Helen asked.

'No.'

'But. . .' Helen's tone was thoughtful. 'Dr McIver's asked you to take a look at her—and Dr McIver's not on duty tonight.'

'I think. . .' Annie hesitated. 'Well, maybe I'd better not say what I think,' she said at last.

'I see.' Helen was momentarily baulked. She looked at Annie and sighed in exasperation. And launched into the grievance she threw at Annie on a weekly basis.

Or daily.

'Dr Burrows, when are you going to do something about your clothes? You could be so attractive if you tried—but, sitting up there, you look about fourteen years old!'

'You think so?' Annie returned Helen's smile, swung her legs some more and allowed herself to consider. Maybe Helen was right. Maybe she did dress in clothes that made her look young. Maybe jeans and oversized checked shirts weren't dignified enough for a doctor.

So. . .should she wear slinky clothes like Sarah? Annie's smile faded. Ridiculous. Clothes like that weren't meant for the likes of Annie Burrows so, if Helen thought jeans and T-shirts weren't dignified enough, maybe she should stick entirely to sensible skirts.

Ugh!

Annie tried a glare at Helen, which didn't quite come off. There was no way Annie could come the dignified, autocratic doctor over Helen. Helen was fifty-something and had been night charge sister here for ever—or maybe longer. There was little round here that Helen didn't see. She was looking at Annie now with eyes that saw far too much.

Well, maybe Helen could be put to use—instead of letting her stand and speculate on thoughts inside Annie's silly head.

'Helen, do you know a Melissa?' Annie asked. 'Are there any Melissas who live locally?'

'There's Melissa Fotheringay. She's five.'

'Wrong age.'

'What age are we looking for?'

'Someone who might be this one's mum.'

Helen's face stilled.

Silence.

Helen stared from the baby to Annie's face—and then back to the baby.

'You mean. . .?' She frowned. 'You mean you really don't know who the mother is? Does Dr McIver know?'

'I don't know what Dr McIver knows,' Annie admitted. 'Helen, keep this to yourself,' she begged, 'but think of Melissas for me.'

'But there's no other local Melissa. The only other Melissa I know—or knew—was Melissa Carnem.' Helen's forehead furrowed in thought. 'Melissa Carnem was a nurse here. She came from Melbourne and left just before you arrived. But. . .'

'But?'

'Well, she's long gone. And Melissa's blonde and blue-eyed and fair-skinned. This little one has such brown curls and lovely brown eyes. . .'

'So she has,' Annie said thoughtfully, and a muscle twitched at the side of her mouth. 'But maybe. . . Helen, maybe she's very like her father.'

Annie's candid grey eyes met Helen's. Woman to woman. A message passed between them that was unmistakeable.

Helen stared incredulously down at the baby, and she saw then what Annie saw.

'You don't think. . .' Helen's eyes had grown so wide they practically enveloped her face. 'Annie, you can't think. . .'

'Helen, were Melissa and Dr McIver. . .friends?'

Helen almost goggled.

'Oh, my dear!' Helen couldn't tear her eyes from the baby. 'Melissa went out with Dr McIver a few times. But. . .'

'Why did Melissa leave?'

'She went to Israel.' Helen was staring at the child with a disbelieving daze. 'Melissa lived in a soap bubble. Full of plans that changed almost daily. In the end, she decided she wanted to live on a kibbutz. Find herself or something. She'd come here because she'd thought living in the country would be wonderful, but she was bored after a couple of months. And she's been gone. . . she's been gone almost ten months.' Helen's eyes fell again to the baby and both women were silent.

Ten months. . .

The silence was broken by the sound of a bell. It took a huge effort for Helen to respond, but the bell rang again and finally she did.

'I'll have to go. That'll be Robert Whykes, needing more pain relief—or more reassurance.'

'The physio's coming tomorrow,' Annie said automatically. 'Tell him that should help.'

'I already have,' Helen told her. 'But the only thing Robert's interested in is an instant cure. He doesn't want to know a damaged disc in a neck can take months to settle.' Helen turned to the door, and then hesitated. 'And, by the sound of it, here comes Dr McIver. Oh, my dear, I'm busting my stays to know what's going on here.'

'You're not the only one,' Annie confessed. 'I think my stays bust about half an hour ago.'

Tom walked in and further conversation was cut short. Helen cast him a curious glance as they passed, tried a smile which didn't quite come off—and retired fast.

He'd entered the room with his customary long stride, but he stopped dead when he saw Annie who was still perched on the couch at the end of the ward, legs swinging. Nestled in Annie's arms, the baby had almost finished her bottle. The child's deep brown eyes were wide open and looking about her with avid intelligence as she sucked.

The likeness was startling!

'It took you a while to tear yourself from Sarah,' Annie commented.

As always, Annie was ignored. To Tom, Annie had kid-sister status. He walked slowly forward, his eyes on the child in her arms.

This was the dearest little baby, Annie reflected, watching Tom's face work through a gamut of emotions. Some babies only a mother could love. This little one, though. . .

The child was perfect. She had lovely dark skin without a blemish, a halo of deep brown curls, bright eyes that gazed up at the world with interest and a tiny, rosebud mouth that sucked at her bottle for all it was worth. And, even when drinking, her eyes seemed to be constantly dancing.

Life was good, her eyes said, and this bottle was fantastic!

Tom stared down and the silence went on and on. The only sound was the slurping sucks made by a hungry baby.

There was only one way to break the silence. Ask the unaskable. Ask what she was aching to know. What had to be voiced some time.

Annie's voice gentled. 'Tom, is this your daughter?'

He heard her then, and took a fast step back. The step put distance between him and the baby—but his eyes stayed on the child in Annie's arms. It was as though the man were seeing a miracle.

'No!' he muttered blankly. 'I mean. . .'

'Can I read the note?'

Tom put a hand to his shirt pocket—and then let it fall again. He looked helplessly at Annie. Tom's face—strongly boned, lined with laughter and intelligence—usually reflected confidence. It was the face of a man at ease with his world. Out to enjoy every moment. But now. . . Annie had the feeling if she reached out and pushed he'd fall right over.

With sudden decision, she slid down from her perch, stepped forward and placed the little girl into Tom's arms.

'Take her.' Her voice was insistent. She lowered her hands so that Tom was forced to grasp the bundle of baby. The milk bottle sagged to one side. The baby gave a last suck at the empty bottle, then turned her gaze up to Tom McIver's face—and smiled.

The resemblance was unmistakable. Carved in stone. And Tom McIver looked as if he'd been punched in his solar plexus.

He stared down into the smiling little face for a long, long moment. The baby smiled and smiled and, despite his shock, the corners of Tom's mouth twitched in response. He couldn't resist her. Who could? And they were matching smiles. . .

A tiny miracle—and she was all Tom's.

She had to know.

Annie lifted the note from Tom's shirt pocket. Tom was too pole-axed to argue. She flicked open the single folded sheet—and stared.

I have a friend who had a baby and went to live on a kibbutz, and it sounded fantastic—a dream. So I conned you into making me pregnant. But then I found it was stupid because kids tie you down and I've met a great guy who doesn't want a baby. So if you don't want her adopt her out. If you want things

signed—adoption forms or anything—my mum will
forward them. Her address is below.

I haven't named her—it seemed stupid when I
didn't want her. They're pressuring me into regis-
tering her now so you name her if you want. I know
I tricked you into making me pregnant so I doubt if
you want anything to do with her but Mum said I
had to give you the choice.

Melissa.

Annie read and re-read the note. Then she looked
into Tom McIver's face. He was shocked to the core.
In his arms the tiny mirror image of Tom gurgled and
chuckled at this delightful world.

Despite the gravity of the baby's situation—despite
the sheer irresponsibility of the unknown Melissa's
actions—for the life of her, Annie couldn't keep the
muscles at the corner of her mouth twitching in
response.

Tom saw.

'Dr Burrows,' Tom McIver said, his voice dangerously quiet as he looked across his tiny daughter at his
partner. 'Dr Burrows, I believe that if you so much as
smile I shall wring your neck!'

'Who's smiling?' Annie pressed her lips tight
together as she fought for control. 'I mean, who could
laugh at this?'

Who, indeed? Certainly not Tom McIver. His daughter was, though. Well fed, warm and content, the baby
was chortling with pleasure.

'Annie. . .'

'I'm sorry, Tom.' Annie forced her features into
something resembling gravity. Tom was right. This was
a nightmare situation. But for the whole eight months
Annie had been in Bannockburn it had been Tom who
had been in absolute control, and a reversal of roles
was something Annie had ached for.

Tom McIver had run the Bannockburn hospital since

it had been built six years before, and he pulled every
string. Annie had been brought in to cope with the work
he didn't want himself, and to give him time to enjoy
himself.

He enjoyed himself all right——but not with Annie.
Annie soon discovered why Tom had chosen her for the
job. It was because he could treat her as a hard-working
doormat. A kid sister with a medical degree. Plain,
hardworking and useful. Nothing more.

'She's competent and ordinary,' Annie had overheard
Tom telling someone the first week of her time in
Bannockburn. 'If we're lucky, she'll grow to be a great
old-maid doctor. She's not the sort to give trouble. The
town will get its money's worth.'

Annie had darn near walked out on the spot when
she'd heard that. Only the thought of how lovely
Bannockburn was, and how much she wanted this job,
had made her stay.

Well, not quite only. . .

There was also the knowledge that, despite his pench-
ant for women who looked as if they'd stepped off the
cover of *Vogue*, Annie had been head over heels in love
with Tom McIver since the first time she'd seen him.

Stupid, stupid, stupid. . .

She should never have come. But she had, and over
the months, as Annie worked whenever Tom wanted
a social life and studied at night while Tom McIver
entertained his stream of beautiful women, she'd started
to smoulder. Tonight things had come to a head. Tonight
she'd been close to handing in her resignation.

Now her anger had been diffused so fast she couldn't
believe it. For once in his life, Tom McIver was totally
at a loss.

'I gather you didn't know of this little one's exist-
ence,' Annie managed, getting a grip on herself with a
massive effort.

'No!' There was anger in Tom's clipped response.

And then he looked down again at his daughter's face—
and the anger faded again to wonder.

'I see.' Annie compressed her lips again, swung herself up to her perch and considered father and child
from a height. 'So. . . What will you do with her?'

What, indeed? Tom stared helplessly down at his
child. His mouth twisted into a grimace.

'I haven't the faintest idea.' Tom shook his head.
'You've checked her? She. . .she looks lovely. Is she
healthy?'

'She's perfect,' Annie said softly. 'Great little body.
Well nourished. No nappy rash or any other sign of
neglect. No problems with her hips or anything else, as
far as I can see. I'd say she had a fairly trauma-free
birth, and she's been well looked after since then.'

'By Melissa's mum, I'll bet,' Tom said savagely,
unconsciously holding the baby tighter. 'It won't have
been Melissa. She doesn't care for anything.'

'You don't like Melissa?'

'No, I do not!'

'Well, pardon me for asking,' Annie said mildly, 'but
why did you make her pregnant if you don't like her?'

Then, as anger grew to near apoplexy on Tom's face,
Annie jumped from her seat and crossed to the door.

'I'm sorry, Tom,' she said softly. 'Of course, it's
none of my business. I'm off to bed now. Goodnight.'

'*Annie*!'

It was a roar of rage, and the baby in Tom's arms
jumped and blinked. Then she smiled again.
Great game!

Annie raised her eyebrows.

'Yes?'

'Annie, you can't just leave me.' The rage was being
supplanted by panic.

'Is there a problem?'

'Of course there's a problem. I can't look after
a baby.'

'You can't look after your own daughter?'

Silence. Annie raised her eyebrows in mild enquiry—and waited.

'*My daughter.*'

Tom said the words slowly, and as he spoke his anger faded. So did his panic. What was left was absolute incomprehension.

'She is your daughter,' Annie said gently. 'I guessed even before I saw the note. Sometimes resemblance between parent and child is so marked that it's unmistakable. It is in this case. Unless you're absolutely sure you can't be the father, I wouldn't waste time DNA testing.'

'But it was only the one night.' Tom groaned and shook his head—shaking off a nightmare. 'I guess... it must have been after the Bachelors and Spinsters Ball. I hadn't had a night off for ages and I'd finally managed to find a locum. I drank too much. Melissa had some damned liqueur she kept insisting I drink. She drove me home and then...'

He broke off, his expressive face working overtime. It showed doubt, then confusion, and finally—anger.

'Hell,' he swore. 'It was Melissa who... She must have meant to get pregnant. She set me up...'

'You can be as angry as you like with Melissa,' Annie said gently, 'but it doesn't alter the fact that the little girl you're holding is your daughter. Whatever her mother's done, Tom, it's not the baby's fault. Now you need to decide what to do with her.'

'Do...' Tom looked down and he groaned again. 'I don't know what to do. *You'll* have to do something. Admit her into the ward here, Annie. I can't look after her.'

'Why not?'

'Because...'

'All she needs are feeds and nappy changes,' Annie said bluntly. 'And I'm rostered on call tonight so you won't be called out. Of course you can look after her.'

'Admit her *here*!'

Annie shook her head 'Tom, she's not sick. The hospital's quiet. There's no one else in Children's Ward and you know, with the layout of the hospital, as soon as we admit a child we have to call an additional nurse. Do you expect Helen to roster on another nurse—wake someone after midnight and ask them to work—just to look after your baby?'

'She's not my baby!'

'Whose baby is she, then?' Annie demanded. She removed her glasses and met his look head on. 'You're the only parent this little one seems to have, Dr McIver.'

'*Annie...*' It was a roar of anguish. 'You have to look after her.'

But even doormats have their limits.

'Tom, I'm going to bed,' Annie told him, hardening her heart. 'Helen will give you enough formula and nappies to last the night. I know something about adoption procedures and fostering so if you'd like to talk to me about that I'll meet you after morning ward round. We'll discuss it then.'

'Annie, stop it,' Tom demanded, his anger flaring. 'Stop it this minute. You're not my damned doctor!'

'No?' Annie looked at him thoughtfully. 'What am I, then, Dr McIver?'

'You're my friend, dammit!'

'And, as your friend, you'd like me to take your daughter and care for her overnight—or until you can figure out what to do with her. You'd like me to take over responsibility for her.'

'Yes.' Tom sighed and his shoulders sagged. 'That's just what I would like, Annie. You've done some paediatric training. I haven't done anything.'

Should she?

No!

For once, common sense prevailed. There was no way Tom McIver was involving her in this, Annie thought bitterly. He didn't think of her as his friend. He thought of her as his doormat. And the doormat had just revolted.

'Yes, you have, Tom,' Annie said gently—inexorably. 'You've fathered a child. This little one doesn't need a doctor. She needs a daddy—and you're it. Welcome to fatherhood, Dr McIver. Welcome to responsibility. Yours. Not mine. Yours.'

'But, Annie. . .'

'Goodnight, Tom.' Annie set her face and hardened her heart. 'Good night. You take care of your daughter. I'm going to bed.'

CHAPTER TWO

IT WAS all very well to say the baby was Tom McIver's responsibility, but it didn't stop Annie worrying. In the few short minutes she'd held her, the baby had melted Annie's heart.

She took her time going to bed. Annie undressed slowly, then sat before the bedroom mirror and stared.

What had Melissa done? Seduced Tom and then tossed away his daughter as if she didn't matter? Her love affair with him had been so casual that she was moving on to the next man without a backward glance. 'I conned you into making me pregnant. . .'

If Tom had made love to Annie. . . If Annie had been privileged to bear his child. . .

Annie closed her eyes—and then opened them again to stare at herself with brutal honesty. What hope would someone like her ever have against the likes of someone like Melissa?

She was too short. Her grey eyes were too big for her face. Annie's nose was snub and there were definite freckles scattered over her nose and cheeks. 'Let's face it,' she told her reflection harshly. 'Compared to Sarah, you're just plain ordinary.'

'So what?' Annie made a face at herself in the mirror and hauled the pins from her hair. Released from its knot, her hair curled round her face in an unruly mass. A brown mass. Mud brown, her mother called it, and sighed every time she saw her.

'I don't know how I came to be stuck with such a drab daughter,' she'd told Annie from her childhood on. 'You take after your father. Thank heaven your sister takes after me. Oh, my dear, your skin. . . And your nose. . . For heaven's sake, just wear plain clothes

22

and have a career where looks don't matter. And dress plainly or you'll make yourself ridiculous.'

Annie made another face and stuck out her tongue at her absent mother and sister. It didn't help. They still had the power to hurt. Her mother was right. Sexy clothes were for the Melissas and Sarahs of this world.

As was the man she loved. Tom McIver.

And Tom's baby.

What would it be like to have such a little one of her own?

Fat chance she had of ever finding out. She was the worker. The sensible, plain one. The doormat. She should block out all thoughts of Tom.

But the baby's smile stayed with her, and she couldn't help worrying, so Annie tossed and turned and listened to the sounds next door all through the night.

First she heard two large dogs being ejected from their master's bedroom. Tom's voice was apologetic but firm.

'I'm sorry, guys. I know you like sharing, but three of us in the bed is crowded and four is ridiculous.'

A few anxious whines—then the whines escalated.

And Tom's voice.

'Look, one day you'll make a couple of nice bitches happy—and your world will fall to pieces, too! Until then you'll just have to accept that women and children come first. Before dogs.'

The dogs weren't in the least impressed. They made their displeasure felt in full chorus, and Annie grinned as she heard Tom placate them with food.

'And you needn't think this is the start of a new routine! It's just for one night. One night!'

What did Tom think would happen tomorrow?

Then Tom tried to put his daughter to sleep while, on the other side of the wall, Annie kept right on listening.

'It's two a.m., dammit. Babies your age are supposed to sleep twenty hours a day.'

Tom's daughter obviously used a different rule book.

From what Annie could hear, the little girl seemed happy as long as Tom held her. It was only when he put her down that she started to cry.

Five times Annie heard Tom say, 'Now sleep!' Then the sound of light being clicked off. Five times she heard fussing, followed by Tom's muffled curses. Gradually the baby's fussing turn to a full-throated roar, the dogs howled in sympathy, the light clicked on again and Tom's distinctive footsteps stomped back and forth. Over and over again.

Finally, at about four, Tom fed his daughter again. In the peace while the baby suckled Annie fell into an uneasy sleep and left them to it.

When she woke the next morning there was silence. Even the dogs were quiet.

Eight o'clock. Today was Saturday and there was a ward round to be done before clinic at ten. Annie dressed for work in a sensible skirt, blouse and white coat—doormat clothes, but at least they made her look older than her jeans—and went to see what the rest of the world was doing.

It wasn't doing a lot. The hospital was Saturday morning quiet. The day nurses weren't busy and the news of the baby's arrival had already spread through the hospital.

Robbie, the hospital administrator—or 'matron', as he jokingly called himself—stopped her as she walked past.

'OK, Annie, what gives?' he growled, and at her look of incomprehension he took matters into his own hands.

Robbie was six feet three, built like a tank and his face was almost hidden by a vast red beard. He was gentleness personified with patients—but when he decided that Annie should talk to him she didn't have much choice. Now he physically lifted her off her feet and set her in his chair.

'Dr Burrows, I can get nothing out of anyone and I

am going nuts,' he growled. 'Did Melissa Carnem really dump a baby on our Dr McIver last night?'

'Rob, it's none of your business.'

'It's none of your business either, but you know. And Pete, my cousin who works at the garage, knows. And Helen. Everyone except yours truly. So give!'

'Hmm.' Annie tried to rise——and got nowhere. 'Rob, I thought nurses were supposed to respect doctors. You know how it's supposed to work. I expect tugging of forelocks and the odd bow and scrape. Pinning the doctor down until she reveals confidential information isn't in any nursing manual I ever read.'

'Well, grow, then,' Robbie ordered. 'I'm damned if I can be deferential to a five-foot-four scrap of a girl who refuses to tell me what I want to know.'

Annie grinned. In medical situations Robbie snapped straight back to being one of the best nurses Annie had ever worked with, but now. . . Well, one of the reasons Annie liked working in Bannockburn was the informality of the excellent staff. The lines between nurses and doctors——so clearly drawn in her big training hospital——were so hazy in Bannockburn you could hardly see them.

'So, what do you know?' she asked cautiously as Robbie glared.

'Melissa filled her car with petrol before she came to the hospital last night,' Robbie explained with exaggerated patience. 'My cousin works the pumps. He recognized Melissa, saw the baby in the back seat and asked what was going on. And she told him. Brother, did she tell him! And my cousin's been shooting his mouth off ever since.'

So, by now, the whole district would know.

'Is Melissa still in town?' Annie asked slowly.

Robbie shook his head.

'Not according to my cousin. She told him she was catching a plane overseas this morning. And Helen wouldn't tell us anything——even when I pulled rank.

And she's bigger and older than you. If I threaten her with physical violence she rings my mum. But. . .' Robbie shook a bewildered head. 'Annie, has she really left a baby with Doc McIver?'

There was no point in dissembling. Robbie had to know sooner or later.

'Yes,' Annie said bluntly. 'She has.'

'And is it his?'

'You'll have to ask Dr McIver,' Annie said primly— and then she watched as Robbie's broad face broke into the broadest of smiles. As the father of three, if there was one thing Robbie loved it was a baby and he reckoned the whole world just ached to be parents.

'Bloody hell!' He stroked his beard and thought things through. 'Where's the baby now?'

'With Dr McIver, of course.' It was hard to suppress a chuckle as Annie watched Robbie grin. 'Where else?' She forced herself back into medical mode with a supreme effort. 'Now, suppose we take a look at Mrs McKenzie's ulcer, Robbie? If it's not looking better today we'll need to consider a graft.' She lifted her patients' case notes from the desk and then, as an after-thought, she collected Tom's as well.

'And I'll take a look at Dr McIver's patients as I go,' she told the bemused Rob. 'He might just be busy this morning.'

'If it's really his baby, he might just be busy for life.' Robbie chortled. 'Oh, boy. . . The valley's going to love this!'

There was an hour's gap between ward round and morning clinic. Annie tried to talk herself into reading the newspaper or doing bookwork—but finally she did what she most wanted. She made a mug of hot, sweet tea and carried it to Tom's apartment.

There was no answer to her knock. Not even the dogs seemed interested in a visitor this morning.

Annie hesitated, then pushed the door wide and went right on in.

The dogs were in the living room. They rose with the reluctance of two weary canines. They'd had a hard night, their exhausted eyes said. Pacing the floor with a baby must be hard work. It was as much as they could do to give their tails perfunctory wags. They were far too tired to be watchdogs.

As they slumped back on their mats Annie crossed to the bedroom door and knocked.

Nothing.

She opened the door just a crack.

Tom and his baby were fast asleep.

Tom's bed was huge. Just plain vast. There was a hospital crib beside the bed but the baby wasn't in it. The little one was right where she wanted to be, sleeping peacefully in the crook of her father's arm. Right against his naked chest.

Annie's heart missed a beat at the sight of them.

As always, Tom McIver had the power to take her breath away. The first time Annie had seen him she'd been a fifth-year medical student and Tom had been giving a guest lecture on country medical practice. He'd only just started in Bannockburn then, and had been brought in to tell the students what they could expect.

His talk had held the lecture theatre enthralled. Even medical students with no intention of working outside a city in their lives had come away enthusiastic.

Tom had talked of his ideals.

He'd talked of the concept of whole care—of taking responsibility for the health of a child at birth and seeing that child grow into adulthood. He'd talked of knowing the ills and troubles—and the joys—of whole families. Being with them in good times as well as bad. Of being part of their lives, and them being part of his.

Tom's talk had convinced Annie that country practice was for her, and Tom's charismatic, caring personality had stayed in her heart ever since.

Now his personality showed through. Tom McIver might be irresponsible—might have sired a baby in ignorance—but now it was impossible for him not to care. It would have been impossible for Tom to put his child in another room last night and let her sob herself to sleep. It would have been against. . .

Against all the reasons why Annie loved him.

Annie stared down at father and child, and she felt the old familiar longings surge through her stronger than ever. If only. . . If only she could be Tom's Melissa. The mother of his child.

'In your dreams, Annie Burrows,' she muttered fiercely. 'In your dreams.'

Tom McIver opened his eyes and stared straight at her.

Annie managed a shaky smile.

'I brought you a cup of tea,' she told him, her words spilling out a shade too fast. 'I thought you might need it.'

'Annie, you're an angel!' Tom pushed himself up on his pillows and held out his free arm. The covers fell completely away, revealing him to be naked to the hips.

Annie blinked—then took three steps forward to thrust the tea into his hand, and three fast steps back.

'I won't bite,' Tom said mildly, and Annie flushed.

'I came to ask what you want to do,' Annie told him, monitoring her voice to keep it emotionless. She kept her eyes on Tom's face—not his magnificent body. 'If you want me to contact social workers it'll be easier if I do it now. After midday on Saturday it's impossible to find anyone.'

'Why would I want you to contact social workers?' Tom asked slowly.

'To look after the baby.'

Tom cast an uncertain glance down at his daughter. 'Yeah, well. . . I've been thinking. Maybe I don't need to. If you look after things here for the weekend I'll take the baby to Melbourne. Find Melissa and sort things out.'

Annie shook her head. 'Not possible.'

'Why not?'

'Because Melissa's catching an international flight this morning. She may already be out of the country.'

Tom stared. 'Says who?'

'Says Robbie's cousin at the garage. He saw her last night and she told him what she was doing.' Annie hesitated, but Tom had to know the worst some time. 'Tom, it seems Melissa told Pete everything. About you and the baby. Everything.'

'I see,' Tom said slowly, in the voice of someone who doesn't see at all. 'So. . .if Pete knows. . .'

'Then the whole valley knows,' Annie confirmed gently. 'They know Melissa brought your daughter here last night. There's no escaping it.'

'I suppose not.'

Tom set his tea aside and sank back onto his pillows, his daughter still tucked against him. The baby didn't stir.

'Well, I know Melissa's mother won't take her,' Tom said bleakly, thinking aloud. 'I met her once. She's a hard-headed businesswoman with a life of her own. I can't imagine her taking on a grandchild.'

'Your own parents?' Annie said gently, and winced at Tom's harsh laugh.

'You have to be kidding!'

'OK.' Annie took a deep breath. 'So it's you or adoption.'

Tom's eyes flew open. 'I guess. . .' He glanced uncertainly down at his daughter. She'd snuggled into him, her tiny body curved into his chest. She looked. . .

She looked as if there was no power in the world that should drag her from where she was.

'It wouldn't be so hard if she didn't look like me,' Tom said slowly.

'I don't suppose it would.' Carefully noncommittal,

Annie stood back and waited. In her brief paediatric training she'd seen this before—the awful gulf facing a parent giving up a part of themselves. And Tom had only just learned that this new little part existed.

Tom shifted again and took a mouthful of tea. He looked up at Annie and then took another mouthful. And another. As if he were gaining strength from the hot, sweet drink. Finally he put the empty mug down. And stared at the ceiling.

'You know the adoption procedures?' he asked flatly.

'You've never had a patient go though it?'

'Never—thank God! Have you?'

'Yes. If you decide. . .' Annie faltered to a halt. She looked down at man and child. They looked so right, the two of them. A matched pair.

Some decisions were just too hard for anyone to make.

'Once you've decided on adoption I'll call in the social welfare people,' Annie said finally. 'They'll arrange foster care. That can be done now, if you like, if I ring before midday.'

'Foster parents? Why not adoptive parents straight away?'

'There's a six-week cooling-off period,' Annie told him. 'You and Melissa must both state you want the child adopted. Then she goes to foster parents and waits. After six weeks you need to re-state your wish for adoption. It'll take longer than six weeks if Melissa's overseas. The forms will be sent there.'

'It seems a lot of trouble.'

'Babies are,' Annie said gently. 'They have to be. They're people and this little one has as many rights as you have, Tom McIver. Despite what Melissa's done, your baby deserves better than just being dumped.'

'I just meant. . .' Tom sighed wearily and finally looked at her. 'There's no need to get on your high horse, Annie. I'm not looking for a quick fix here.'

'Aren't you?'

'Well. . .' Tom sighed again. 'I don't know,' he said honestly. He looked down at the baby in the crook of his arm, and touched her gently on the nose. Then he looked up again at Annie and his face was almost pleading. 'Are you telling me, Annie, that *my daughter* has to stay with foster parents for six weeks?'

My daughter . . .

Annie blinked. The way he said it. . . There was pain behind the words—the pain of impending loss.

'Foster parents are special people, Tom,' Annie told him, her voice gentling even further. 'You know that. They're carefully chosen to take good care of her.'

'Yeah, but. . .' His voice trailed off to silence.

Tom's baby was still deeply asleep. She hadn't stirred as Tom had pushed himself up on the pillows to drink his tea. She'd slept as he'd touched her and she slept on now. Tom stared down at her for a long, long moment, and the expression on his face was one Annie had never seen there before.

'Annie, she hasn't even got a name,' Tom said bleakly, with an ache behind his voice. 'She's six weeks old—and my daughter hasn't even been given a name.'

'Then maybe it's up to you to name her.'

'But if I do that. . .'

'If you name her then you're laying claim to her.' Annie still kept her voice carefully noncommittal. She was trying desperately to keep herself objective. Unemotional. 'Tom, I know this has been a shock, but you either have to dissociate yourself and pass her on fast to people who'll love her—or you have to start making decisions.'

'Decisions?'

'Like whether you want to name her. Whether you want access to her as she grows up. Whether you want her to know you as her father.'

'If I have access she'll know I didn't want her,' Tom said bitterly. 'What sort of father would I be, demanding access? She'll know I didn't even want her conceived.'

'She'll know that, anyway,' Annie said bluntly, 'if she's adopted.'

Tom stared up at Annie for a long moment—and then slumped wearily back down on his pillows. Cradled in his arm, his tiny daughter slept peacefully on. She'd probably sleep all day now, Annie thought ruefully, and then wake up and socialize again tonight.

It didn't have anything to do with Annie. This baby was *not* her responsibility. So why was she feeling exactly like Tom?

She had to get out of here. She must. . .before she walked over and lifted the baby from Tom's arms and burst into tears.

Which wouldn't help anyone.

'Tom, I must go,' she faltered. 'I've done ward rounds of your patients as well as mine but there are people waiting in clinic. There's no need for you to work today. I can cope on my own. Do you. . . Do you want me to ring the social worker now—or wait until Monday?'

Tom glared and his hold on his daughter tightened. As if Annie was threatening to take her away.

'Thank you for doing my rounds—but I haven't decided.'

'OK.' Annie nodded. 'Are you prepared to look after her for the weekend?'

'I don't know whether I can.'

Annie bit her lip. 'Tom, if you want her to go to foster parents today then the latest you can leave it is eleven-thirty. Let me know before then—OK? You know where to find me.'

With one last uncertain look at the tiny child nestled against her father's chest, Annie walked out and left Tom, staring after her. His face was a picture of absolute confusion.

And, if anyone had seen her as she walked down the corridor, so was Annie's.

*   *   *

Annie was removing plaster from Henry Gillies's foot when Tom made up his mind. He burst into Annie's surgery, causing both Annie and the elderly Henry to jump.

'Annie, she's staying!'

Annie lowered Henry's foot carefully onto the examination table and turned to face Tom. Dressed now in tailored trousers and neat shirt, newly shaved and his hair almost ordered, Tom McIver looked much more civilized than the last time Annie had seen him.

But no more in control.

'Would you like me to come out and talk to you?' Annie offered, directing a pointed look down at the all-too-interested Henry.

'No.' Tom shook his head. He strode forward and gazed down at Henry's foot with interest. 'The whole valley must know what's happening by now, and Henry's a mate. Rebecca told me you had Henry in here, Annie, so I knew you wouldn't mind me interrupting. What have you been doing to yourself, Henry?'

'A blasted cow stood on me foot,' Henry told him. 'Happened last week. You were out with some damned woman or other so Doc Burrows shoved plaster on it for me. Now she says this plaster's gotta come off and she'll stick more on. If you'd done it you would have stuck on some that'd last, wouldn't you, Doc?'

Tom smiled down at the elderly farmer. His smile was engaging and mischievous. The old Tom McIver.

'Don't you trust our Dr Burrows?'

'Well, she's all right,' Henry said grudgingly. 'For a woman. But this bloody plaster. . .'

'Has to come off.' Tom lifted Henry's foot and inspected the old plaster with care. 'Dr Burrows is right, Henry, and I'd have done nothing different. The bruising to your foot takes ten days to go down, and when it does the plaster becomes too loose. You'd be wiggling your toes no end if we left you in it.'

'Yeah, well—they itch,' Henry growled.

Then Henry saw what Annie was lifting from the bench. His eyebrows hit his hairline and he visibly recoiled. 'Hell's bells, girl! I dunno about that. A circular saw for a plaster. . . What happens if you get carried away?'

'I fix your itch for good!' Annie chuckled and relented. 'It's OK, Henry. The saw might look vicious but it doesn't spin. It simply vibrates and shakes the plaster apart. If it touches your skin you'll hardly notice.'

'Hardly notice as my foot falls off. I see.' Henry had the look of a man appalled. He cast a look of appeal at Tom. 'You trust her with that?'

'Absolutely.'

'Bloody hell!' Henry shook his head in disgust. 'Women and power tools! What next?' He sighed. 'Go on, then. Take the bloody thing off. And if the foot comes off with it, well, I've got another one after all, and I'm not a man to grumble.'

He put his hands behind his grizzled head and, blocking out the thought of Annie behind a buzz saw, looked up at Tom in resignation. 'So what are you saying, lad? That you're keeping this baby I've been hearing about?'

'Well. . .just for a short while. Are you right to start, Annie?' Tom cast Annie a sideways glance, then held Henry's foot while Annie positioned the saw. 'Just for the six-week waiting period until I can get her adopted.'

Annie was concentrating on what she was doing so she was halfway into the plaster before she thought about what Tom was suggesting. Then she had to raise her voice above the noise.

'You mean—keep her here instead of sending her to foster parents for six weeks?' she asked.

'That's right.'

'And then get her adopted straight away.'

'It'd be simpler.'

'Then, no,' Annie told him bluntly. 'No way.'

'No?' Tom's brows snapped up.

'Hold the foot still, Dr McIver,' Annie rebuked him, smiling down at Henry. 'Even though Henry has two feet he probably wants both of them.'

'That's told you, Doc.' Henry grinned broadly, relaxing. 'She's a good 'un, our Doc Burrows. Bet none of those painted dolly-birds you take out have the guts to tell you off.'

'Thanks, Henry,' Tom said dryly, frowning, but he did concentrate then. They didn't speak until the plaster fell away. Tom started cleaning the leg while Annie fetched bandages and prepared the new plaster.

'What's wrong with her staying here?' Tom asked, his tone almost conversational. 'I've thought it out. She can stay in Children's Ward and I'll personally pay for an extra nurse if there's no one else in. That way she doesn't have to go to strangers.'

'Tom, to your daughter you're a stranger.'

'She's used to me already.' Tom grinned and there was a hint of pride in the smile. 'When I handed her over to Cook just now she cried.'

'Lucky Cook.'

'The hospital's quiet,' Tom said firmly. 'Mrs Farley doesn't mind.'

Mrs Farley wouldn't if Tom asked it of her, Annie thought bitterly. No woman would. All Tom had to do was smile. . .

Well, someone had to say no to him.

'Tom, it's not on,' Annie told him. 'If you want your daughter adopted then she has to go to foster parents. There's a six-week cooling-off period and that cooling-off period can't start until you no longer have custody.'

'You mean. . .if I keep her here for six weeks then there still has to be six weeks of fostering after that?'

'That's right.'

'OK.' Tom dried Henry's leg and dusted it off. Automatically he took the bandages from Annie and started winding. 'We can get round that, I reckon. If she's admitted here then I don't have custody.'

Annie stared. 'You're saying you'll admit her here and then tell the social workers you're not caring for her?'

'No.' Tom shook his head. 'I can see they wouldn't come at that. But if you admitted her, dearest Annie. . . If she was in your charge. . .'

And he flashed her that all-persuasive smile.

His 'Annie-the-doormat' smile.

'He's wheedling you, girl,' Henry commented dryly. 'Don't you let him talk you into what's not right, Doc Burrows. Doc McIver does the best wheedle I've ever been privileged to hear. He even talked Bert Humphrey into giving up the fags!'

'He does, doesn't he?' Annie agreed, glaring at Tom. 'It works a treat—most times. But now. . . Tom, you're asking me to lie to the social workers to get you what you want.'

'Not lie. . .'

'The six-week cooling-off period means no access. So I'll be lying unless you promise not to have any access at all to your daughter,' she told him bluntly. 'That means not even standing on the other side of the observation window and looking.'

'Annie. . .'

'I won't do it, Tom,' Annie told him. 'Wheedle all you want.' She stared across at him, troubled. Half of her would really like to see this man grow attached to his small daughter. But the other half was the doctor in Annie, who'd gone through the adoption procedures with patients and knew the heartache on all sides. . .

'Tom, as soon as the cooling-off period begins the welfare people start the process of finding adoptive parents. Those parents may have been waiting for a baby for years. They'll be told about your daughter and asked whether they want her. They'll be told there's still a possibility you'll change your mind, but if nothing changes in six weeks then the baby is theirs.'

'So what's wrong with that?' Tom's hands still

wound Henry's bandages, but he was working totally
on automatic. He stared up at Annie, a trace of defiance
on his face.

'Because the reason the welfare people have stirred
up so much hope—have told a desperate couple there's
a baby—is that they'll believe you've taken the hardest
step of all. You've relinquished your daughter. And
unless you have, Dr McIver, then it's just not fair. So
don't ask it of me, Tom. I won't do it.'

Tom's face darkened. 'What is this, Annie? Some
sort of moralistic punishment?'

'I'm not punishing anyone,' Annie said strongly.
Dear heaven, she hated saying this. But it had to be
said. 'Tom, I can't punish some childless couple who'll
want her desperately.'

'You're saying there's a possibility I won't give her
up in six weeks?'

Deep breath.

'If you keep seeing her I believe you may not.'

'Well, that's nonsense. Of course she has to be
adopted.'

'So why won't you give her up now?'

'Because I've only just met her,' Tom said harshly.
'Hell, Annie. . . Six weeks. . .'

'You want to get to know your daughter better?'

'Yes, I do. Is there something wrong with that?'

'You'll get to know her—and then give her away?'

'Yes.'

'Oh—ho. . .' Henry broke into their conversation.
The elderly farmer was lying on the procedures trolley
with the look of a man thoroughly enjoying himself.
'If you think that then you don't know babies, Doc
McIver. When mine were born they were so ugly I
pretty near had a palsy stroke but, ugly or not, they
pretty soon wind themselves round your heart like a
hairy worm.'

'Henry, this is—'

'No matter about sleepless nights,' Henry continued,

watching Tom's bewildered face and sweeping aside protest. 'The house'll be chaos. The wife and every other busybody in the neighbourhood'll be clucking over seven pounds of squawking sog. You can't get a word in edgeways. Cooked meals are a thing of the past.

'Then the wife says, "You hold her for a bit," and the kid looks up at you and you see your eyes in her eyes. And she smiles. And they tell you it's wind but you know for sure it's nothing of the kind. She's grinning at her old man—and she's got you hooked for life.'

Henry's eyes crinkled and he chortled in pure delight.

'And I wouldn't mind betting it's happened already,' he said slowly, watching Tom's face. 'What do you reckon, Dr Burrows?'

Annie took a deep breath—and somehow managed to avoid Tom's eyes as she looked back down at Henry. Henry was a wise old farmer who saw a lot. And she saw it, too.

There was nothing else to do but to tell it to Tom like it was.

'Well, I reckon. . .I reckon you're absolutely right.' Annie managed a smile. 'I think Doc McIver needed to hear that, and it's better coming from a man. Like women can operate power saws without chopping off toes, you men can fall in love with your babies.'

A sideways look at Tom's thunderous face made Annie decide her best bet was a fast retreat.

'Henry, I have people in the waiting room and, seeing Dr McIver's free, I can leave you safely with him.' She gave Tom an uncertain smile. 'I've finished with the power tools now, Dr McIver. It's safe for you to take over.'

She walked out the door before Tom could say a word.

CHAPTER THREE

ANNIE worked steadily through a stream of patients all morning and didn't see Tom again for hours.

In fact, her patients were all suffering minor ills, but consultations were lengthened by every single patient's enquiries as to what was going on with Dr McIver's baby. In the end, Annie was starting to suspect there'd been hasty assembling of symptoms just to grill her!

Every time there was a knock on the door she looked up, expecting Tom to burst in and tell her to contact the welfare people. There was no Tom—and by the time Annie saw her last patient it was two o'clock and she knew that Tom would be spending the weekend with his daughter.

'He's not admitting her into the hospital under my bed-card,' she told herself firmly. 'If he thinks he can talk me into caring for her. . .'

Feeling uncharacteristically crabby, Annie bade farewell to Rebecca, her receptionist, and turned her thoughts to lunch. It had been a long time since breakfast. In fact—looking back—Annie couldn't remember breakfast at all.

Drat Tom McIver and his emotional high jinks, she thought bitterly. He had her on an emotional roller-coaster. She wished the man would just go away! She stomped crossly around the back of the hospital to her apartment, opened the door—and saw Tom McIver in her living room.

So was his baby.

The cot was fair in the middle of the room, and Tom's daughter was soundly asleep under the covers. Tom had just emerged from the kitchenette, carrying a bowl of salad.

Annie stared down at the table. Two places were beautifully laid on a linen tablecloth. There were wine glasses and wine in an ice cooler. Crusty bread rolls. There was a smell of something cooking in the kitchen that made Annie's nose wrinkle in appreciation. Beef. Bacon. . .

Good grief!

'Whatever you want, you can't have it,' she said, and watched Tom's face crack into a grin.

'Annie, you are the most untrusting woman. . .'

'I know you, Tom McIver.' Annie stalked back to the door and held it wide. 'Out. No, no and no—and out!'

'Annie, I need to talk to you.'

Yeah. He wanted her to be a doormat. She just knew it.

'Then organize a meeting in the clinic.'

'Annie. . .' Tom plonked down the salad bowl in the middle of the table and walked toward her. He placed two hands on her shoulders and held her at arm's length.

Only Annie knew what the feel of him touching her did to her.

But Tom was oblivious. He was intent on something—but Annie didn't know what. She only knew she didn't trust him one inch.

'Annie, this is the first taste of my new domestic self,' he told her. 'Hannah and I have been to the butcher's and the greengrocer's and we've spent the rest of the morning cooking.'

'Hannah?'

'Hannah.' For the first time a trace of uncertainty crossed Tom's face. 'I. . . I've named her Hannah. After my grandmother.'

'It's pretty, Tom,' Annie said gently—and somehow she managed to wrench herself from his hold and take two steps back. 'Do you want it to be a permanent name?'

'I guess. . . The adoptive parents will be able to change it, I suppose.'

'They can,' Annie agreed. 'But. . .you're not agreeing to separation yet?'

'Monday,' Tom told her. 'I figured if you wouldn't
agree to keeping her here longer then I'd at least have
her until then.'

'I see.' Annie met his look head on. There was still
something going on. Something Tom wanted. 'So, what
do I owe lunch to, then, Tom?'

'It's a goodwill gesture.'

'No.'

'What do you mean—no?'

'Meaning, no, I don't believe you,' Annie said flatly.
'What do you want?'

'At least have a glass of wine before I ask.'

'No again. I don't drink when I'm on call.'

'One glass won't hurt.'

'And I especially don't drink when someone's trying
to con me into something against my better judgement,'
Annie said ruthlessly. She shrugged off her white coat
and tossed it onto a chair. 'So tell me.'

Tom stared at Annie for a long moment and then a
faint smile played at the corners of his eyes. 'No, Annie,
I won't,' he told her firmly. 'I've taken a great deal of
trouble to set this up so the least you can do is to eat
my lunch. And it's delicious,' he said persuasively.
'You wouldn't want Tiny and Hoof to have it all.'

Annie glared, glared again and finally caved in.

She was hungry. It did smell good. And she knew
enough of Hoof and Tiny to know, once offered, her
meal would be gone in seconds.

'I'm making no promises. I owe you nothing.'

'Just shut up and eat like a good doctor,' Tom said
blandly. 'And then we'll see!'

So Annie sat and ate a magnificent casserole and
enjoyed every minute of it, but all the time her eyes
demanded to know what he wanted. She loved being
with Tom. She always did. But she didn't relax for a
minute.

Finally Tom pushed his plate back and sighed.

'You're a very unrestful woman, Annie Burrows.'

'If I rest then I'm taken advantage of,' Annie said darkly. She glared across at him—and then relented enough to smile. 'OK, Tom. You've fed me well and I've enjoyed it. If I can help I will—but not in looking after your daughter for six weeks.'

'Just for tonight.'

Silence.

'Tonight?' Annie said blankly.

'It's the hospital ball, remember?' Tom said. 'And Sarah's expecting me to take her. And you're on call, anyway.'

'You want me to babysit Hannah tonight?'

'Well. . .sort of.' The rat had the grace to look embarrassed.

'If I'm on call I can't look after a baby.'

'No. But I've talked to Robbie and there's a nurse willing to cover Children's Ward. Chris. So all you have to do is say yes.'

'Tom, you only have your daughter for two more nights.' Annie shook her head, confused. 'And you want to spend one of those nights going to a ball with Sarah?'

'I can't cry off. Sarah's already fed up with me,' Tom admitted, 'because of last night. . .'

'I don't see why she should be,' Annie said waspishly. 'She had a good enough time before midnight.'

Tom gave Annie a strange look. 'Annie. . .'

'What?' Annie's crabbiness, having receded a little in the face of Tom's food and infectious smile, flooded back in force. This man was asking her to babysit his daughter so he could take another woman to a ball!

Dear heaven. . .

How could she keep living in Bannockburn? She was crazy to stay. Crazy—when she was head over heels in love with a man who didn't even know she existed.

Except as a medical partner-cum-baby-sitter!

'Annie, I can't afford to get Sarah offside,' Tom said slowly. 'She's a lovely girl.'

'Lovely, all right,' Annie flung at him bitterly. 'With the brains of a cotton-wool ball.'

He gave her another strange look. 'She's a school teacher, Annie.' Tom looked at her steadily. Under his gaze, Annie felt herself blush.

Well, OK. Maybe she was being unfair. It was only the woman's laugh that went right through her. And the fact that Tom thought she was lovely. She swallowed. 'You're. . .you're serious about Sarah, then?' she asked in a small voice, and winced inside as Tom nodded.

'I think I am.'

'I see.' Annie rose and carried her plate to the sink. Then she stood with her back to him. Asking questions like this was like probing a raw wound, but she had to ask. 'It was someone else last week, though, wasn't it? Sarah's new on the scene.'

'Yes, but. . .'

'But?'

'As I said, Sarah's a school teacher,' Tom said softly. 'She's good with children. Maybe if I could persuade her. . . Maybe she'd take Hannah and me on.'

Annie wheeled round, her face incredulous.

'You're thinking of setting up a family?'

It was Tom's turn to blush. 'Well, yes. It did occur to me. I thought. . .if I could spend some time with Sarah tonight. . . Think about it. Get her to think about it. I mean. . .' Tom spread his hands helplessly, rose and walked over to his sleeping daughter. He stared down at the baby for a long, long moment—and then looked back at Annie.

'She looks like me, Annie,' he said tightly. 'Hell. . .I can no more look after a baby than I can fly—but Henry's right. She's got to me.' He shrugged. 'Look, call it a crazy idea but I have two days to think about this. Two days. So. . .I already know I'm starting to love my daughter. Now I need to spend some time with Sarah.'

'But. . .you don't know whether you love Sarah?' Annie was striving for all she was worth to keep her voice casual.

'Well. . .' Tom considered. 'I don't think one loves a wife like. . .well, what I'm starting to feel for Hannah. I mean. . .it's different, isn't it? I've always thought the bit about romantic love was overrated. If you're wise you choose your marriage partner sensibly.'

'And Sarah's sensible?'

'I think so.'

'And beautiful, to boot.' Annie grimaced. 'Very sensible, Tom McIver. Poor Sarah!'

'Hell, Annie. . .' Tom's face darkened in anger. 'What am I supposed to do?'

'I have no idea,' Annie snapped. 'No idea at all. I'm sure what you're intending is very sensible and you'll all live happily ever after. So don't let me stop you. OK. Tonight I'll take responsibility for your daughter while you go and sweep the lovely Sarah off her feet and talk her into a life of domestic bliss.'

'There's no need to be a cat.'

'No!' Annie hauled herself up to her full five feet four inches and glared for all she was worth. This man was so blind! How could he not see he was tearing her heart out? How could he stand there and say there was no such thing as romantic love—when Annie was so in love with him she was even agreeing to his crazy schemes for finding a wife?

'No, there's not,' she agreed, 'so I'll go back to being a doctor. Sensible, hardworking, plain Dr Burrows, who's always there when you need her. And who's crazy enough to say she'll take responsibility for your daughter. For tonight and tonight only!' She stalked over to the door and held it wide. Tom was looking at her as if she'd taken leave of her senses.

Maybe she had.

'You'd better. . .you'd best leave me to study in peace before the next call comes,' she faltered, 'because I need space. But, yes, I'll take responsibility for your baby, Dr McIver. Once only. But as for the future. . .'

She shook her head and couldn't go on—and her face grew bleak.

Who knew what the future held? Bannockburn and Dr McIver. Dr McIver with Mrs McIver and their child? Living next door for ever?

No and no and no! She'd have to leave.

'As for the future, your future is up to you,' Annie said dully. 'Your future with your baby has nothing to do with me. *Nothing.*'

She held the door wide until Dr McIver and Dr McIver's baby were gone.

Saturday night started quietly.

Annie was reinserting a failed drip in the next-door ward when Tom and Sarah brought Hannah to Children's Ward. They made a stunning couple—Tom tanned, self-assured and impossibly handsome in his dinner suit, escorting a vibrant Sarah. Sarah with legs that went on for ever and blonde hair that swung down in a silken veil. The figure-hugging crimson dress she wore—slit to the thigh to reveal miles of leg—was simply stunning.

They were enough to take an onlookers's breath away, smiling at each other as they stood holding hands over the crib as they admired the sleeping Hannah—and then sweeping off to the ball.

While Dr Annie Burrows—Cinderella Burrows—stayed behind and tried hard not to turn into a pumpkin.

'Don't they look just so lovely together?' Chris, the night nurse on children's Ward, sighed romantically as she watched them go. 'They're made for each other. Oh, Dr Burrows, if only I looked like Sarah. . .'

'Yeah, well, that makes two of us, dreaming for the moon.' Annie dug her hands deep in the pockets of her

white coat and surveyed the empty corridor with gloom.
The lovely, laughing pair had left and the emptiness in
the little hospital without Tom's presence was almost
tangible.

Annie wrinkled her nose, readjusted her glasses and
managed to grin at Chris. 'Well, we can't all be Snow
White. And we're not exactly the ugly sisters. It's only
that Sarah's so gorgeous she'd make Sleeping Beauty
look seriously in the looking-glass.'

'Boy, you know your fairy tales,' Chris said in
mock awe.

Annie shrugged and smiled, her natural good humour
surfacing. 'Well, I guess there's an up side here, Sister.
With most of the town at the ball, we should have a
nice peaceful Saturday night. And you have a whole
night of looking after a children's ward with one only
healthy patient.'

'Isn't it great?' Chris chuckled and hauled a romantic
novel from her apron pocket. 'And I know just what
I'll do with it.' She sighed and sank into an easy chair
beside Hannah's cot. 'Bother fairy tales. I've something
better. Bliss! Off you go and enjoy your quiet time, Dr
Burrows, and don't find me any patients to spoil my
peace. I'm up to page one hundred and twenty and
if Jack doesn't fall into Kimberley's arms tonight he
may never!'

He didn't.

Half an hour later Murray Ferguson, aged eight, was
brought in, suffering a severe asthma attack. Chris's
romance was put good-naturedly aside, and she and
Annie worked solidly for two hours, stabilizing the little
boy's breathing.

Then Ray Stotter was admitted with chest pain. Annie
and Helen were fully occupied for another two hours
while they ran a full barrage of tests on the old man,
decided he was most likely suffering from severe
angina, started him on glyceryl trinitrate and reassured
his terrified wife that, while Annie was fairly sure that

the pain was not from a heart attack, she was keeping him in overnight to be safe.

In the end, Annie spent more time with Martha Stotter than she did with her husband. For once Helen's soothing presence didn't work, and it was Annie the elderly lady clutched as she sobbed out her fears.

It was one in the morning before Annie ended up back in Children's Ward to check Murray's breathing. Murray was asleep but Hannah was awake and starting to fuss.

Chris was walking the baby back and forth across the ward, soothing her and watching Murray's fitful sleep at the same time.

'She won't settle,' Chris told her. 'There's nothing wrong, but every time I put her down she sobs her heart out. Maybe she's missing her mum.'

'I suspect she's just worked out a routine where nights are for play,' Annie explained wearily. 'Maybe that's what pushed Melissa into abandoning her.' Annie stared down at the tiny baby in Chris's arms and her heart wrenched. Maybe that was the explanation—but how could a woman walk away from her own child? Walk away and leave nothing but a note, disclaiming all responsibility?

'Poor little mite.' Chris cradled the little one closer, echoing Annie's thoughts. 'She's such a lovely baby, and she looks so much like. . .' She shook her head. 'Well, I always thought Melissa was an air-head and now I'm sure of it. And heartless as well. Meanwhile. . .'

'Meanwhile we just keep one baby as happy as we can until the grown-ups in her life sort out the mess,' Annie said sadly, and Chris nodded.

'Well, she's fed and happy enough now—as long as I don't put her down. I don't want Murray to wake. He's terrified.'

'The worst of his asthma attack seems to be past now, but it must be dreadful, not being able to breathe,'

Annie agreed. She frowned at Chris. 'Can you cope here?'

'Of course I can,' Chris assured her. 'I can cope with two patients with my hands tied—and while one of them's asleep it's a cinch.' She grimaced and then grinned. 'Pity about Jack and Kimberley, though.'

'They'll still be just as passionate tomorrow night.' Annie returned her smile. 'The good thing about a hero in a book—you can shove him under the bed until you're ready for another spot of passion. Much tidier than real life romance.'

'I wouldn't know,' Chris said darkly. 'I've a feeling romance'd be more fun as a hunk of fabulous male who refuses to be shoved anywhere!' She looked at Annie thoughtfully. 'Anyway, Dr Burrows, I've been dying to ask. I have the odd romantic fling—though usually it's so odd I retire to my romance novels fast—but you. . . You haven't been out with anyone since you came here. Don't you want to?'

Annie shrugged. 'I'm busy,' she said. 'I don't have much time. . .'

'You're pretty, though,' Chris said, considering. 'If you got rid of those glasses. . .'

'Then I couldn't be so fussy about choosing males.' Annie grinned. 'I couldn't see them.'

'Yeah, well, that might be an advantage,' Chris said gloomily. 'The problem with working in this hospital is that you keep seeing Dr McIver, and every other male pales in comparison. Don't you think he's gorgeous?'

'Gorgeous.' Annie's voice was flat and devoid of expression—and Chris's eyes widened.

But in her arms Tom's baby stirred and fretted, and with one last long look at Annie's mounting colour Chris resumed her walking.

'OK, miss,' she told the baby. 'You just shut up and listen to Aunty Chris tell you the story of her love life. That'll put you to sleep if anything will.' She grinned at Annie and carefully forbore to comment on Annie's flushed face. 'Just don't find me anything else to do, huh?'

Of course, Annie did.

Ten minutes later, just as Annie was climbing into bed, the phone on her bedside table went.

Helen.

'Annie, there's a car accident coming in,' Helen said briefly. 'I don't know the details but ETA is ten minutes.'

'I'm on my way.'

There was no more to be said. Annie was already moving. She dressed quickly. This was the worst time. The ambulance officers rang as soon as they received a call, but they wouldn't know yet what the damage was.

And if it was bad. . .

Trauma in a place like Bannockburn could be even more of a nightmare than it was in the city. In the city there was specialist back-up on call. Here. . . Well, it was thirty miles by ambulance to the nearest major hospital. There was only Annie and Tom.

In Bannockburn there were no strangers. Road victims weren't statistics. They were the people you passed every day in the street. Friends.

'Let it be minor,' Annie breathed as she dressed. 'Please. . .'

Two minutes later Annie was dressed and hurrying down the hospital corridor to Sister's station. Helen was replacing the phone as Annie arrived, and her face was grim.

'It's bad,' Helen told her, her fingers already flicking through the phone lists of nurses on call. 'It's Rod and Betty Manning and their little girl, Kylie. Rod and Betty had been to the ball, and they collected Kylie from the babysitter on the way home. Then they hit a tree.'

'They're alive?'

'Yes. But Rod and the little girl look grim. Betty has facial lacerations. That's all I know. Dave says Rod was unconscious at first and now is screaming in pain, and Kylie's leg was caught. They've had to cut her free. Dave sounds really churned up.'

Annie nodded. Dave was one of the valley's team of volunteer ambulance drivers. He'd done basic training but the few times he'd been called out hadn't been enough to give him a thick skin against trauma.

'Staffing?' she asked. Helen knew staff availability far better than Annie.

'I'll need Chris as back-up in Theatre,' Helen said, thinking aloud, 'and I've called in Susan to take over the wards. I'll call in Elsa to help in Children's Ward—she's done SRN training and should be able to cope with Murray's asthma. I don't know, though. . .' Helen's face clouded. 'Tom's baby's still awake. Maybe I should ring Robbie—but he's tired and he's on tomorrow.'

'We don't ring Robbie because of Tom's baby.' Annie frowned. 'But you're right. Elsa can't cope with the baby as well as Murray.' The thought of the easily flustered Elsa trying to calm Murray as well as care for a sobbing child made her wince. Told to sit by Murray's bed and monitor his breathing, Elsa would be fine—but Annie didn't want her distracted by a baby. 'Is Tom back from the ball yet?'

'He came in a few minutes ago.' Helen cast a dubious look at Annie. 'I think he and Sarah are in Tom's apartment. But. . .' Helen looked doubtful. 'I was about to phone Tom. We'll need him here, won't we? He won't be able to look after his. . .the baby.'

'Yes, we'll need him,' Annie agreed. 'But Tom told me Sarah was good with children.' Annie managed a wry smile. 'I guess. . . Well, there's no choice. Let's see how good!'

Annie wheeled Hannah's cot straight round to Tom's apartment. Tom took two minutes to open the door to Annie's knock—and there was lipstick on his collar again.

Annie shouldn't notice such trivia, but she did. She couldn't help it.

Forget the lipstick, she told herself dully. Concentrate on what matters. Annie pushed the baby inside the apartment before Tom had a chance to protest. Both Tom and the dogs stood back, stunned.

'Dr McIver, you're needed in Cas.'

Tom blinked. And so did Annie.

Sarah was there. She stood in the middle of the living room, her lovely blonde hair dishevelled, and on her face there was the dazed look of someone who'd been... Well, someone who'd been doing what Annie longed to do. Why did it hurt so much? Why couldn't she be impartial and unemotional and...and *sensible*?

Just do what had to be done, say what had to be said and get out of there. She pushed Hannah's cot forward until it was in front of Sarah.

'We need you too, Sarah,' she said. 'Tom needs you to look after his baby. It's an emergency. I hope you don't mind.'

'Emergency?' Tom's eyes creased into swift concern. Sarah might look dazed, but Tom's mind was razor sharp and clicking fast into medical mode.

Annie turned to face him. Look at his face, she told herself. Not the lipstick.

'Car accident,' she said briefly. 'Three—two adults and one child. ETA about now. I have to get back.'

'I'm on my way.' Tom was transforming from lover to doctor with the speed of light.

'But, Tom...' Sarah's voice was a wail of dismay. 'Tom, you invited me back for coffee. Can't Annie cope by herself?'

'No,' Tom said bluntly, and Annie knew he'd hardly heard Sarah's wailed protest. He was concentrating only on what lay ahead.

'Not with three badly injured people, I can't.' Annie relented a little at the look of dismay on Sarah's face. What she was doing wasn't fair, Annie acknowledged. Even though she couldn't help calling Tom away, how would Annie feel if she'd been Sarah. . .in Tom's arms. . .?

Some wish!

'I'll take over by myself again as soon as I can,' she promised the disappointed woman. 'If the injuries aren't severe Tom can come back. . .'

'But—'

'But I'll be a while, Sarah.' Tom was hauling off his dinner jacket and tie as he spoke. In a sense Annie knew that Sarah had already been abandoned. Tom's thoughts were no longer here—with this woman—but concentrated solely on medicine. His capacity to block everything else out when he was needed—to devote himself absolutely to the job at hand—was one reason why Annie loved him, but Sarah saw it as no virtue.

'Well, I'll go home, then,' Sarah said sharply. She hitched her handbag over her naked shoulder with an irritable flounce. 'There's no point in me hanging about.'

Annie looked from Tom to Sarah and back again. Tom was hauling on his white coat, and Sarah was looking petulantly at Tom. Neither of them was seeing the cot.

Both of them had to face it. Both of them had to face the responsibility of one small baby. If this was an embryo family then the time to start was right now.

'Sarah, Tom needs you to babysit,' Annie managed, and she was pleased that her voice sounded firm. 'Tom, you know we can't spare staff to look after a well child. Hannah will scream the hospital down if she's unattended. So. . .'

Annie looked from Sarah's beautiful, discontented face to Tom's blank one.

'So someone has to look after your child, Tom.' And somehow she forced her eyes to stay steady.

After all, it wasn't up to her to find babysitting answers here. It was Tom's job. It was his baby. And Sarah was his intended bride.

Annie had made a suggestion, and that was all she could do. She was needed elsewhere.

'Come as soon as you can,' she managed, and Annie turned—like the coward she was—and left them to it.

Give her car accident injuries any day!

Annie didn't know how he sorted it out. She didn't ask. By the time Tom arrived in Casualty—about three minutes later—Annie was drowning in work. So were the three nurses. Tom walked to the casualty entrance and involuntarily recoiled.

Annie breathed a sigh of relief as she saw him. Kylie Manning, five years old and terrified, needed more doctors than just Annie. Annie checked the saline drip, gave the child's hand a squeeze of reassurance and straightened.

'OK, Helen,' she told the charge nurse as Helen moved in to take her place beside the child. 'Dr McIver's here. Could you and Dr McIver get Kylie into X-Ray?' As Annie spoke she walked swiftly to another trolley, where Chris was trying to stop a distraught woman from rising. 'It's going to be fine, Mrs Manning.' Annie pressed the woman's shoulders gently onto the pillows. 'There's no need for distress. We're looking after Kylie and she'll be OK.'

Then Annie's eyes sent an urgent message to Tom— a message that sent him straight to the child's stretcher. Get the little one out of here, Annie's eyes said. Annie wouldn't be able to settle the mother while the child lay blood-spattered and semi-conscious within sight.

'Are you right with everything else?' Tom asked rapidly, his eyes taking in the three trolleys in quick succession before he focused on the child.

Annie wasn't. Mrs Manning was bleeding from a deep and ragged laceration on her forehead and was obviously in shock. On another trolley her husband was writhing and moaning with pain. Dave, the ambulance driver, had his work cut out to hold the man still.

'I'll settle Mrs Manning and then I'll see to her husband,' Annie reassured Tom, but her reassurance was meant mostly for Mrs Manning. 'Kylie's broken her leg, though, Dr McIver, and she'll need an X-ray...'

Once again Annie's eyes met Tom's. They'd always worked brilliantly together, intuitively understanding what was needed and reacting in tandem with the ease of partners of years. Now a flicker behind Tom's dark eyes showed he understood. Helen lifted the sheet covering the child's leg for Tom to see. One look, and Tom's face tightened.

There was little circulation below the knee. A compound fracture had cut off the blood supply. If Tom didn't move fast the child would lose her leg.

'But Rod...' The woman Annie was holding sobbed in distress, tears mingling with blood. She tried to push Annie away. 'My husband... He's worse than me. Can't you see...? Can't you hear...?'

'Rod has a broken arm,' Annie told her. 'We'll stop the bleeding from this cut first—'

'But—'

'We say what comes first, Mrs Manning,' Tom said briskly, his voice cutting across her husband's moans. 'Dave is looking after your husband. I suggest you lie back and let us get on with our jobs as fast as we can.' And, with a long, hard look at Rod Manning, Tom wheeled the child out of the room.

'I'll be with you as quickly as I can,' Annie murmured after him, knowing Tom needed her now. The child needed two doctors but successful triage—sorting of priorities—was impossible.

Annie couldn't go while Betty was bleeding so badly. And her husband? One brief inspection had shown a broken arm, but Dave said the man had been fleetingly unconscious. That meant he needed a more thorough examination.

So, although Kylie was number one, only one doctor could be spared for her as yet—and Tom's fast actions said he agreed with her. Blessings on Tom. There was no one Annie would sooner hand the child on to.

'OK, now, Mrs Manning,' Annie told the young mother, gently wiping the blood from her face and checking the pressure pad over her wound. 'You know Kylie's in the best of hands. Dr Tom will take good care of her. She has a broken leg and that's the worst of it, as far as I can see, so we'll tend to you next. Let's get you into our procedures room and stop that face bleeding.' She lifted the pad over the woman's forehead and winced.

Mrs Manning looked fearfully up through shocked and pain-filled eyes. 'You're sure. . . You're sure my little girl. . .'

'Tom won't let Kylie die of a broken leg,' Annie said firmly, and watched the fear fade out of the woman's face. And then the fear flooded straight back as Betty looked over to her husband.

'But what about Rod?'

'Apart from a fractured arm, I don't think there's anything major wrong with your husband,' Annie told her. 'And it seems a simple break.' It was hard to keep harshness—the censure—out of her voice.

If what Annie suspected was true. . .

If she was right then she couldn't set his arm tonight, nor could she give him much in the way of pain relief. Annie motioned to the nurses and ambulance officer. 'Susan and Dave will look after your husband. Then, as soon as you let me stop your face bleeding, I'll see to him. So what about lying back and letting me give you something for the pain so I can get on with my job? You agree, Mrs Manning?'

'OK. You'll tell me if anything. . .'

'We'll tell you what's happening every step of the way,' Annie said strongly. 'Promise.'

Thirty minutes later Annie was free to join Tom. He and Helen had Kylie in Theatre. As Annie pushed

through the doors Tom looked up from injecting anaesthetic, and his face cleared at the sight of her. His
old-maid partner.

'Great. We're losing the little circulation we have. I
was just about to make do with Helen.'

'And double great.' Helen sighed her relief. In an
emergency Helen could give an anaesthetic—coached
every step of the way by either Tom or Annie—but
she'd only been called on to do it twice and she'd hated
every minute of it. Now she stepped back from the head
of the table and made way for Annie.

'The leg. . .' Annie's voice was fearful. If the artery
was torn there was little hope. It took the air ambulance
two hours to make a return trip to Melbourne to the
nearest vascular surgeon.

'The artery's not torn. There are bone fragments kink-
ing the artery and a small amount of blood is still getting
through. I may be able to manipulate the leg back so
the artery can do its job.'

Annie looked doubtfully at the leg. Dear heaven, it
was a mess. If Tom could do that. . .

'How are things out there?' Tom lifted his hands and
Helen slipped surgical gloves over his long fingers as
he snapped the question at Annie.

Annie didn't answer straight away. Her first priority
was the anaesthetic. First she checked Kylie's general
condition. The child was already deeply asleep and intu-
bated. Her vital signs were OK—as well as could be
expected in a child as shocked as this. The monitors
were attached and everything looked fine to go.

'Better,' she told Tom finally, signalling him to go
ahead. 'Rod's been X-rayed. I'm pretty sure the only
thing wrong with him is a broken arm—radius and
ulna—and a few bruises. He's confused and is still
making a heck of a fuss, but he's been lucky. Chris is
specialling him.'

'And Betty?'

'She's lost a lot of blood, mainly through that gash

on the head. It's taken a bit of stitching to stop the bleeding and I'm afraid my handiwork will be temporary. She'll need repair work by a plastic surgeon. I've sedated her now. Susan's watching her but I think she'll sleep until morning.'

'Which leaves Kylie,' Tom said grimly. 'Two have been lucky. Let's see if we can make it three out of three.' He stared down at Kylie's leg. 'Hell. I could use an orthopedic surgeon here.'

They certainly could. Annie stared down at the fractured mess that was Kylie's knee and knew the child was in for major reconstructive surgery.

The time for that would be later. A skilled children's orthopaedic surgeon would take over where Tom left off—but if Tom couldn't establish a blood supply now there'd be nothing for the surgeon to reconstruct.

'OK, Dr Burrows,' Tom said steadily. He looked at Annie, meeting her eyes and demanding her full concentration. Whatever else had happened tonight—whatever drama was in Tom's life and whatever other patients waited for them outside—this was the time to focus totally.

To commit themselves to saving one little girl's leg.

CHAPTER FOUR

IT WAS an hour before Tom was sure he'd done it. He'd lifted fragments of bone, shifted the leg, applied traction and watched. Three times the blood had surged into the lower leg—only to slowly cease. And Tom had sworn softly and started again.

It was a further half-hour before he stood back from the table, wiped sweat from his forehead and said in a voice where exhaustion dragged, 'That's it. The best we can do. Let's hope it's stable enough to hold.'

Annie looked down to where the child's feet—untouched and unharmed—lay side by side. Completely normal—until Annie looked higher and saw Tom's massive dressing around the knee. . .

'There's circulation now,' Annie told Tom gently. 'You've done the best you could do, and I doubt a skilled orthopod could have done better. But she'll need an artificial kneecap and months of physio.' She hesitated. 'Will we send her on to Melbourne tonight?' She took the reversal injection from Helen and carefully inserted it, then watched like a hawk as the child's muscles came into play. Any minute now Kylie would try to breathe on her own.

'Let's keep her tonight and stabilize her as much as we can,' Tom said wearily, as Helen moved to take his tray of instruments away. 'I don't like the idea of moving that knee one bit.' He looked down at the little girl's face, his eyes concerned. 'She's got a hell of a road ahead of her.'

'At least she has a chance of full recovery.' Annie watched carefully as Kylie's chest heaved. The reversal taking effect, her body retched in rejection of the breathing tube and Annie slid out the hose. Two ragged, painful breaths. . .three. . .and Annie relaxed. Job done.

Thank God!

Annie wasn't the only one glad it was over. Tom's face was grey with exhaustion. The surgery he'd done had required every ounce of his skill and a lot more. He looked absolutely drained.

This was the Tom McIver his women never saw, Annie thought. The Tom who gave every inch of his dedication to his patients. A lesser doctor would have put Kylie in an air ambulance tonight and not tried. . . Not tried because the chances of success were slim. But Tom had fought and Kylie had a good chance of keeping her leg because of it.

Tom was some doctor!

Some doctor. Some love. . .

Dear heaven, she loved him so much. It was as much as Annie could do not to walk over and place her hands on his face and smooth away the lines of exhaustion and pain. Tom did feel this child's pain, she knew. This was the reason she'd fallen so deeply in love with him. He felt his patient's pain like his own and she wanted. . . oh so badly. . .to take his pain and to share it.

She couldn't. Of course she couldn't. It wasn't her place. Annie was part of Tom's medical life—but not a part of his private life at all.

'I'd better go out and see how Rod is.' Unaware of the gamut of emotions tearing at Annie, Tom sighed and crossed to the sink. 'If he's still making a fuss. . .' Tom turned on the taps and let the water flow over his wrists, as if drawing strength from the flow. 'I gather you're not suggesting we set his arm tonight, Dr Burrows?'

His eyebrows rose, and Annie nodded.

'I don't think I'd be game to give him an anaesthetic. I'm guessing as yet, but it's my bet his blood alcohol's somewhere over point one,' Annie told him. 'Maybe a lot higher. I can smell beer and the police asked that I take a blood sample.'

'Have you?'

'I'll do it now.' Annie shrugged. Taking blood samples for the police wasn't one of her favourite jobs but she had no choice. 'I didn't have time before but they're insistent, and when I said they'd have to wait they seemed happy enough. The sergeant says he doubts a few hours' delay will drop him to the legal limit. The tree Rod hit was beside a straight stretch of road, and Sergeant Grey says the wheel marks are all over the road. He must have been drinking heavily at the ball.'

'I didn't notice him,' Tom said shortly.

Annie nodded. Of course he hadn't. What man would notice anything when he had the lovely Sarah in his arms?

Tom wasn't thinking of Sarah now, though. He stared down for a long moment at the child on the operating table and when he turned back to the sink his face was dark with anger. He hauled the tap further round with a force that sent water down so hard that it splashed over onto the floor. Tom didn't notice.

'Bloody fool,' he said bitterly. 'Idiot! To drink himself stupid, and then put his family in the car and drive. . .' He shook his head. 'The man doesn't deserve a daughter.'

'He nearly lost one,' Annie agreed.

Helen had taken the used instruments into the sluice room. Now she came back and looked at Tom, her face creased in concern.

'But you'll treat your daughter better than this, Dr McIver?' the nurse asked gently, and Annie almost gasped. It was a question that had been playing at the edges of her own mind, but she'd never have voiced it. Not in a million years. The redoubtable Helen, however, had no such qualms.

Tom looked up and stared at Helen, but his stare was blind. It looked straight though her.

'I. . .' He shook his head, as though clearing a fog. 'I won't have a chance. My daughter's being adopted.'

'So you say,' the nursing sister agreed equitably. 'Well, let's hope she's lucky enough to end up with parents who don't drink and drive.'

'That's ridiculous. The adoption criteria are rigid.' Tom's voice was curt. He was holding himself under control with a visible effort and Annie could sense his tension growing by the minute.

The pressure of tonight's operation had come on top of almost overwhelming personal pressure, Annie realized. In the moment it took to dump a baby on his doorstep Tom's life had been transformed—and Dr Tom McIver was taking his transformation hard.

'She'll get good parents,' he said tightly.

'Adoptive parents don't come with any guarantees. No parents do.' Helen's voice was implacable. She glanced at Annie, as though seeking silent support for what she was saying, and kept right on talking. 'Rod Manning would pass adoption criteria. To the outside world he's a model citizen. There are whispers that he gives Betty a hard time, but she won't admit that and there'll be no official record that he drinks too much.'

'What are you saying, Sister?' Tom demanded angrily, and Helen spread her hands.

'Just that it's in the lap of the gods who gets your daughter once she's up for adoption, Dr McIver,' she told him, her voice flat and definite. 'And whoever adopts her will have absolute control. You'll have none. No say at all.'

Helen paused—and then shrugged and continued. In for a penny, in for a pound, her body language said. And Annie watched, spellbound.

'Dr McIver, since last night I've been thinking about your little daughter most of the time and. . .well, I've four children myself and I'd find it impossible to hand that responsibility to anyone. It's incredible that Melissa has—and I find it even more incredible that you should.

'You think about it well before you hand your daughter over for life. You'll spend the rest of your days not

knowing what's happening to her. If you can't offer her
a decent life then you don't have a choice—but you're
a grown man with a stable life and. . .' Helen took a
deep breath and glanced at Annie. 'And your pick of
lots of ladies who'd love you and love your daughter.
Some who I bet you haven't even thought of yet.'

Then, as Tom's brow snapped down and he opened
his mouth to retort, she cut him off. 'I'll take Kylie out
to Recovery and watch her,' she told both of them, and
she turned her back on Tom's anger. 'But, Dr McIver. . .
if I were you I'd think long and hard over what you're
doing. Adoption's a final step—and she's so much your
daughter. . .'

Helen directed a shamefaced grin at Annie—as
though she suspected she'd had no right to say what
she had, but was willing to stand by her words anyway—and she wheeled Kylie to the door.

'Oh, and, by the way, Dr McIver,' she added kindly,
turning once more to face him as the door started to
swing closed behind her, 'I'd turn off that tap! Your
feet are getting all wet.'

Tom and Annie were left alone.

'Hell!'

Tom stared at Annie for a long moment and then,
finally, turned his gaze to the tap. The water had been
spraying up and over the bench while Helen spoke. The
overboots on Tom's shoes were soaking and there was
a pool of water around his feet that was spreading by
the minute. 'Hell!' said Tom again, only louder, and
turned off the offending tap.

'It is, isn't it?'

Annie didn't look at him, concentrating fiercely
instead on unfastening the ties on her gown.

Tom stood stock-still and glared. 'How would
you know?'

It was an angry demand—and Annie blinked. Tom
was glaring straight at her.

'I beg your pardon?' she managed, confused.

'You heard,' Tom snapped, lashing out. 'What the hell would you know, Dr Burrows? You just march into my life and dump my daughter on me and then expect. . .'

Annie took a deep breath and finally met his eyes.

'I dumped. . .?'

'You dumped,' Tom threw at her. 'If it weren't for you. . .'

'I didn't dump,' Annie gasped. 'Melissa dumped. If it weren't for me, your daughter would be lying in a hospital corridor waiting for you to stop making love long enough to find her.' Annie tilted her chin and glared. 'Of all the arrogant, rude—'

'You enjoyed dumping her on us yesterday. And again this evening. . .'

'Enjoyed! What was I supposed to do?' Annie put her hands on her hips and let her temper sail sky-high. A part of her knew Tom's tension was so great it had to explode. Part of her was offended, but part of her relished rising to his bait. The relief of a successful operation—of averting what could have been a tragedy—was having its effect, and a good shout would do her good. So. . .a good shout was what Tom got.

'We needed every nurse tonight, and you know it,' she flung at him. 'And your baby didn't need a nurse. I hardly had time to advertise for babysitters.'

'You could have tried.'

'Oh, sure,' Annie snapped. 'Mrs Stotter's here, staying the night with her sick husband. Maybe I could have woken her and asked her to look after your daughter. Is that what you wanted, Dr McIver? Or did you expect me not to interrupt you—to let Kylie lose her leg— because you wanted to spend the night with your precious Sarah? Well, unfortunately, Kylie only has two legs, Dr McIver, and she needs them both—and you have your whole future to spend with Sarah.'

Unexpectedly, Tom's face fell. The anger went out of him in a rush.

'No.'

But Annie wasn't prepared to let her temper go. Not yet. She was actually enjoying herself.

'I don't know what you mean by that, Dr McIver,' she snapped. 'You and Sarah seemed to be getting on like a house on fire when I interrupted you.'

'Yes, and we might have. . . You stopped us. . .'

'Stopped you from ending up in bed?' Annie demanded crudely. 'Well, maybe I stopped you making another baby, Dr McIver. Bully for me and the birth control movement.'

'No,' Tom snapped. 'You stopped me asking Sarah to. . .' And he didn't continue.

Silence.

Annie knew instinctively what he'd been going to say. She could see it in his face.

She knew.

'I stopped you proposing?' Annie asked at last. And her temper somehow faded, too. Just when she needed it most. Dear heaven. . .

'That's right.' Tom's hands ripped through his dark hair and his look of fatigue deepened. 'I had it all planned.'

Annie bit her lip. She mustn't care. She mustn't!

'Well, now's your chance again, then,' she managed, forcing her voice to stay light. 'I can cope by myself now. I'll contact the air ambulance and have them collect Kylie and her mum in the morning, but meanwhile I can hold the fort until dawn. You go back to your. . .'

She stopped as the word hit her, but then she forced herself to say it. The sensation was like biting down on a broken tooth. 'You go back to your family, Dr McIver. Your. . .your family. They're waiting for you.'

'They're not my family.'

'No?' Annie shrugged. She was very close to tears but she was holding them back somehow. Somehow. . . 'Dr McIver, you have a fiancée and a baby. That sounds like a family to me.'

'They're damn well not a family!' Tom lifted a towel and started drying his arms. He looked over at Annie and his normally confident face held a plea for help. 'I tell you, they're not! Annie, what the hell am I going to do?' he demanded. 'What the hell. . .'

Annie stood immobile where she was. If she crossed to the sink. . . If she took one step nearer Tom McIver she'd be compelled to place her arms around his neck and comfort him. . .kiss away the worry and tiredness and uncertainty in his eyes.

She'd told herself over and over that she couldn't even think of such a thing. It wasn't her place!

'Tom, go and ask Sarah to marry you,' she said dully. 'A delay of a couple of hours won't make a difference. If that's what you've decided.'

'That's what I *had* decided.' Tom's voice was as flat as her own. 'It made sense a couple of hours ago. But, then, when you left Hannah with us. . .'

What had gone wrong? 'Sarah wasn't very happy, was she?' Annie asked gently, and waited. And waited. While Tom's tired face grew dark.

Finally he threw the towel on the floor in disgust.

'She wasn't,' he told her. 'Sarah said she spends all day every day with children and she didn't expect to be dumped with my kid on a date. She said. . .she said you were a manipulating little vixen, just trying to separate us.'

Annie blinked. Sarah was. . .jealous?

That was ridiculous.

'Yeah, well, you told me it was my fault you got landed with Hannah,' Annie said mildly, and watched Tom's face crease in disgust.

'Hell, you know I didn't mean that, Annie,' he said. 'You know I was just letting off steam. And you weren't really offended. You never seem to mind. I don't know. You understand. . . But. . .' He shook his head. 'Sarah said you were out for the main chance. . .out for me. . . As if these last two nights haven't been anything other

than a disastrous coincidence that's made you interrupt
us. She said you were trying to split us up.' He shook
his head as though the idea was crazy.

Which it was, Annie thought bleakly. As though
Sarah could possibly think Annie could be any compe-
tition.

'Maybe Sarah was upset, too,' Annie said softly, and
heaven alone knew the effort it cost her to be nice.
'Maybe. . .'

'Maybe,' Tom said wearily. 'Maybe, like me, she was
just ripping back in frustration. She agreed to babysit
Hannah in the end and she'll be back in the flat when
I finish here. But. . .' Once more, his hand ripped
through his dark hair. 'But it's made me see one thing.
I certainly don't know Sarah well enough to marry her.
Hell, Annie, I know you better than I know her. I could
as soon marry you. . .'

He gave the towel a ferocious kick that sent it flying
out to the sluice room, then cast Annie one last unhappy
look—and walked out of the door.

Back to Sarah, and back to his baby.

I could as soon marry you. . .

The words echoed round and round the empty theatre,
and it was all Annie could do not to weep.

'But you certainly wouldn't want to marry me,'
Annie said gloomily to the empty room. 'No way, Dr
Tom McIver. Not in a million years.'

Not ever.

She closed her eyes—and then she started cleaning
up and getting on with the rest of her life.

The air ambulance took Kylie and her mother to
Melbourne at seven the next morning, and Annie was
asleep five minutes after the plane took off. The night
shift was over. Tom could take over medical duties for
the day. Annie didn't care whether Hannah had kept
him awake or if he'd spent the night making love to

Sarah—she was so tired she could hardly hold her head up, and from seven Tom was officially on duty.

She hit the pillows and didn't wake until one. Until someone knocked on her door.

Still mostly asleep, Annie fumbled her way to the door. Tom stood in the corridor, holding his daughter in his arms. He took a step back as Annie opened the door, an expression of almost sheepish apology on his face.

'I thought you'd be awake.'

'I wasn't,' Annie muttered, and folded her arms over her breasts—a gesture of pure defence. Tom was fully dressed in his casual trousers and shirt, and Annie was anything but fully dressed. Her nightie was too flimsy by half and she'd been too tired to do it up properly when she'd fallen into bed. It was too late now to retreat and find a dressing-gown.

Tom was staring. His apologetic expression was changing to one of interest. As if he was watching a frog that had just changed into a princess, or a pumpkin into Cinderella. . .

'I've never seen you with your hair down,' Tom said slowly, his gaze raking her from her bare toes up. Annie's soft brown hair was a cascade of curls around her breasts and her wide grey eyes seemed huge without her normal barrier of glass and tortoiseshell rim.

She blushed crimson and took a hasty step back inside her apartment. She grabbed her glasses from the top of the bookcase and shoved them down on her nose.

Shield up!

'Why don't you wear contact lenses?' Tom asked curiously—and then looked more closely at her glasses. 'They're not very thick. Do you need to wear them all the time?'

Annie's blush deepened.

'Yes, I do need them—and I don't see the point of contact lenses. What do you want?'

Tom's face lightened into a grin. 'Just to annoy you,

of course,' he told her. 'And I'm good at it. I seem to make you cross, without even trying.'

'Not true,' Annie snapped, glaring. 'How can you say "without even trying" when you are very, very trying?' She glanced at her wrist-watch and her glare deepened. 'Tom McIver, the agreement today was that you'd do the work from this morning and I'd take over again tonight. So go away! Unless there's an emergency, I'm not working today and, no, I'm not babysitting.'

'Why do you always attribute my motives to anything but altruism?'

'I didn't think you even knew what altruism meant,' Annie said bitterly. 'Consideration for others is hardly your strong point. And now you appear at my door, holding a baby.' Annie glowered. 'It's enough to make anyone suspicious.'

'Well, I'm not asking you to do anything,' Tom retorted, with the air of a man much maligned. 'The hospital's dead quiet again. You got Kylie and her mum off OK with no problems. I assume if there were any worries you would have woken me.'

'Mmm.' Annie recrossed her arms and wished again for a wrap. Standing in her doorway with bare toes and a nightgown that was way too thin was making her extremely uncomfortable. She wanted her sensible clothes, a white coat and any other defence she could muster. 'There was a doctor on board the air ambulance so they were in good hands. I did think of waking you but—'

She broke off. She'd thought of waking Tom, but the thought of disturbing him. . . If Sarah was still there. . .

She didn't know if Sarah had stayed the night and she didn't want to know. Such knowledge was more than Annie could bear. Anyway, she could hand over patients and histories as well as Tom could. Surgical notes could be faxed later if required.

'You should have.'

'Yeah. . .' Annie put her hand pointedly on the door-knob. 'Was that all you wanted to say?'

Tom ignored the gesture. 'You decided not to send Rod with his wife and daughter?'

'I did.' Annie tilted her head and glared, sensing criticism, and Tom's smile deepened.

'All right, Touchy. I'm not being critical. I just wondered whether he'd wanted to go. He's belligerent as all heck now, and threatening to sue if anything happens to his wife and daughter.'

'He was vomiting as the plane left,' Annie told him. 'Moaning and vomiting at the same time. I gave him as much prochlorperazine as I dared but the alcohol is just going to have to wear off itself. His nausea would have kept the plane's staff from Kylie and Mrs Manning. Mrs Manning needs a plastic surgeon. Kylie needs an orthopaedic surgeon and Rod needs to dry out. The drying-out can be done here.'

'You think it might take a while?'

'The way his body's reacting, his blood alcohol content must be sky-high.' Annie shrugged. 'The police will have a field day with the results of his blood test, but I can't help that. Also, with that level of alcohol on board, his arm will have to wait until tomorrow to be set. Unless you're prepared to give an anaesthetic?'

'No way.' Tom shook his head. 'I'm with you.'

'When he recovers from drunkenness Rod Manning is going to feel really sorry for himself,' Annie said sadly. 'As soon as the result of his blood test comes through the police will take his licence, and there's no way he'll get it back before a court case. He'll be visiting his wife and child courtesy of bus travel, and Kylie's going to be in hospital for quite a while.'

'Months, at a guess.' Tom's smile faded completely. He stared at Annie—and then looked down at his own daughter. 'Fool. . .' He looked back at the girl holding the door open. 'Anyway, Annie, I didn't come to talk to you about work. I came to ask you to go on a picnic.'

'What—today?'

'Today.'

'You're on duty,' Annie said flatly, still deeply suspicious. Tom McIver didn't ask Annie for dates. He asked her for favours.

'Not a far picnic,' Tom explained patiently, 'a near picnic. It's just. . .' He checked Annie's look of stunned incredulity and grinned. 'Hell, Annie, I'm not asking you to fly to Africa or indulge in a spot of illicit drug-running—or even go to bed with me! It's just a picnic.'

Annie's eyes narrowed.

'But why?'

'Does there have to be a reason?'

'Yes.'

'I've told you before—you have a suspicious mind.'

'It's the only protection I have,' Annie said bluntly. 'And I'm keeping it suspicious. You propositioned me with lunch yesterday then asked me to babysit, and now you're offering me food again. What do you want this time, Tom McIver?'

'Not to waste a picnic.'

Annie took a deep breath and watched Tom's face. 'I. . .I see. Sarah. . . Sarah doesn't want to go?'

'You could say that.' Tom sighed. 'Annie, there's a great spot where the river runs into the sea, not much more than a mile from here. If the hospital beeps me I can be back in three minutes.'

'Your favourite seduction site, in fact.'

Tom's eyes narrowed. 'Annie, why the hell are you so aggressive? You sound a real little moralist.'

'Yeah, well, maybe I am.'

'It's what you look like in your nice, sensible clothes with your hair hauled back and your glasses on,' Tom said. 'But you can't sound like a moralist as you look now. Did you know the buttons over your breast are unfastened almost to your waist?'

She didn't.

Annie's blush turned to fire-truck red and she grabbed

the door. Tom prevented her closing it by simply shoving his foot in the crack.

'I'll collect you in fifteen minutes,' he said firmly. 'Wear your bathers under your sensible clothes, Dr Burrows. I dare say your neck-to-knees will look pretty bulky under your knee-length skirt and straitlaced blouse, but Hannah and I will turn a blind eye.'

'I am not going to lunch. . .'

'But—' Tom threw in his trump card '—we have a whole lobster.'

'A whole. . .' Annie gasped and was silenced.

The local lobster went straight to the Japanese export market and the Japanese, with their strong yen, seemed to eat more lobster than Australians did. It was now priced ridiculously high.

'A whole lobster,' Tom said again.

'But. . . Tom McIver, do you know how much lobsters cost?'

'I ordered it yesterday,' Tom said sadly. 'I'd never proposed before—and it seemed like the right thing to do. If things had gone according to plan I'd be an engaged man by now.'

'And you'd be eating lunch with your fiancée.'

'That's right.'

'So. . .I'm a fiancée substitute.'

'You make a cute one.' Tom grinned, unabashed. 'I hadn't realized how cute until now. And, instead of offering you half my worldly wealth, I'm offering you half my lobster.' His amazing smile—never absent for long—flooded back in force. 'Take it or leave it, Annie, but there's champagne as well, and vol-au-vents with Atlantic salmon, avocado salad, chocolate éclairs. . .'

'That's not a seduction scene for one fiancée,' Annie gasped. 'You'd get a whole harem for that.'

'We don't want a harem, do we, Hannah?' Tom said morosely to his daughter. 'We just want Annie.'

'You want me because there's no one else available.'

'Yeah, well, we thought that, didn't we, Hannah?'

The man was at least honest. An honest toad! He looked back at Annie—and his smile twinkled out again. 'But that was before we saw the undone buttons. And what's underneath them. Very fetching! But, if you like. . .if you like, we'll try very hard to forget what we've seen and we'll have a very chaste lunch on the beach. A business lunch, if you like. A business lunch with lobster and champagne. I wonder if I can claim it as a tax deduction. What do you say, Annie Burrows?'

What did she say?

She knew darned well what she should say. She should slam the door hard and go straight back to bed. She'd had six hours sleep and it wasn't enough. And it wasn't the least bit sensible to go anywhere near this man on a social level.

But Annie looked up and saw the twinkle lurking behind Tom McIver's eyes—and she also saw a hint of panic. Tom's life was changing dramatically and he couldn't cope. Not on his own.

And she couldn't refuse.

'OK, Tom McIver,' she faltered. 'I'll. . .I'll be your substitute fiancée for the day. But that means I drink champagne and I eat your lobster and I sunbake. It does not mean I take any calls for you, or babysit your daughter. Or do anything at all for your dratted dogs. Right?'

'Well. . .'

'Right, Tom McIver?'

'I've never had such an ungracious acceptance to an invitation,' Tom complained, and Annie wrinkled her nose and grinned.

'Well, this is what you get! Me! Suspicions included. Take me or leave me, Dr McIver, but I come with conditions. No medicine, babies or dogs. Now, do you want me—or not?'

Tom looked at her with a very strange expression in his eyes, an expression that said he was seeing someone he'd never seen before. Annie Burrows without her defences.

'I rather think I do,' he said slowly. 'And maybe. . . maybe with or without conditions.'

CHAPTER FIVE

As PICNICS went, it was a picnic to die for. Tom had packed everything possible for a magnificent engagement celebration.

The only thing was. . .it wasn't quite your standard romantic scene. Annie checked out Tom's car and she could see why Sarah had whisked herself back to her schoolroom. Tom's Rover was packed high with food and drinks, rugs, cushions, baby capsule, nappy bag— and two huge dogs squashed somehow one each side of the baby capsule.

'They had to come,' Tom told Annie warily, interpreting her look of astonishment. 'I've kicked them out of my bedroom. I can hardly kick them out of my life.'

'I can see that.' The dogs had their dopey heads out of the back windows. Their tongues were almost down to ground level and they were clearly bursting with anticipation. 'Does Hannah like dogs, then?'

'Who could help but like my dogs?' Tom said smugly. 'They're great guys.'

'Yeah, well. . .'

'You don't like them?' Tom sounded astonished.

Annie considered. The dogs' huge heads were bobbing up and down like sprung toys. Their tails were thumping on the car roof and their tongues were leaving a series of damp trails on the paintwork.

'I have to say I've seen brighter dogs,' Annie admitted at last, smiling to take the edge off her criticism. 'These two seem. . . Well, the lights are on but maybe no one's home?'

'Hey, Annie!' Tom's face grew shocked. 'Hell, they'll hear you. What a thing to say about my beautiful boys! I'll have you know their pedigree's impeccable.'

'But are they trained to do anything but bay at the moon?' Annie demanded, and Tom gave a reluctant grin.

'Well. . . They eat on command.'

'I'll just bet they do.'

'And they're house-trained!'

'You mean they know how to sleep on your bed. It's a wonder there's room for you. Honestly, Tom, why didn't you buy yourself a couple of chihuahuas? Let's face it—doorstops would be more useful than these two. Also, they'd eat less.'

'I didn't buy these two,' Tom confessed. 'One of my old patients died last year and Hoof and Tiny were his. They were going to be put down if I didn't take them, and they. . .well, they looked at me. . .'

They looked at him.

That silenced her.

They'd looked at him and Tom had been lost. Of course.

Did Sarah know this side of him? Annie wondered. The side Annie had seen the first time she'd met the man—the side of his nature Annie recognized almost intuitively.

Tom McIver appeared to the world as hard and capable and. . .and womanizing. Inside he was pure marshmallow. Any wife of his would have to be prepared to open her house and heart to all sorts of waifs and strays.

So. . . Where did that leave Tom now? How could Tom give his beautiful daughter up for adoption to strangers when all two stupid, overgrown dogs had to do was look at him?

They hardly spoke as Tom drove the short way to the sea. They couldn't. The dogs barked with joy the moment the engine started and didn't stop until they reached the river mouth.

Once there, the dogs burst out of the car to chase gulls and Annie rubbed painful ears. Tom lifted Hannah's

borrowed baby capsule onto the river bank, then produced so many things from the back of his car that
Annie figured this was a conjuring act.

'Whew. . .' Annie stared down at the ice cooler, holding French champagne, and then gazed up at Tom in
stupefaction.

'This is some seduction scene,' she said slowly, as
she sank onto the pillows Tom had spread over the rug.
And then she looked up at him suspiciously. 'Are you
sure you want to waste it on me?'

'I don't know.' Tom bent to prise open a container
holding lobster. He placed it before Annie and then
he straightened. The lobster cast its distinctive aroma
upward and Annie's nose twitched in appreciation.

Tom stood beside her, his denim-clad legs splayed,
the warm, sea breeze ruffling his tousled brown hair
and his strongly boned face showing uncertainty as he
looked down at the slight girl at his feet. 'I thought I
did,' he said slowly, 'but now I'm not sure.'

Annie was hardly listening. The sight of Tom's body
standing right above her was doing strange things to her
insides—but her attention was almost diverted. Lobster!
She leaned over, lifted a morsel and bit. Mmm. . .

'Well, you can't change your mind now.' She smiled
up at him, then grabbed the lobster container and held
on like grim death. 'At least, not until I've finished this
lobster. And why should you, I'd like to know?'

'You like lobster, then?' He grinned.

'Offer me a lobster or a Rolls Royce and I'm the one
sitting on the road stuffing her face.' Annie returned
his smile and cracked some shell. 'But you can have
half. Did you bring scales so we can make it fair?'

Tom's smile faded. He stood, looking down at her
and considering, and Annie knew he wasn't thinking
of lobster.

'Annie, will you tell me why you're wearing those
clothes?'

'What do you mean?'

'Annie, this morning I thought inviting you on a picnic was a sensible idea.' Tom shook his head, confused. 'Then, when I saw you in your nightgown with your hair down and your glasses off, I thought inviting you was a fantastic idea. But now. . . Now it just seems sensible again. Annie, why are you wearing your jeans and baggy T-shirt? And you've hauled your hair back too tightly again. It's like. . .it's like you're deliberately hiding yourself.'

Annie flushed. He was right, she supposed. They were an ill-matched pair. Tom looked like a hero straight out of a romantic movie, but Annie didn't fit the bill as a heroine.

She was a doctor. Not a lover!

'It's the way I like it.'

'But your hair's beautiful out. Gorgeous.' He bent to touch it but Annie flinched. She concentrated fiercely on her lobster and tried hard to ignore him.

'Tom, this lobster's fabulous. Eat some before I forget the half deal.'

But Tom's attention was not to be diverted. For the first time in eight months he was seeing Annie as a woman, and now he was checking her out from the toes up.

'You know, jeans and floppy T-shirts are for kids. Especially when you're asked out on a date.'

Annie bit again and glowered. 'You decide what you wear, Tom McIver,' Annie said crossly. 'Leave me to wear what I want.'

'But. . .why don't you wear something attractive? Dresses and things. Or. . .even jeans and tops that fit!'

Annie shook her head, her courage slipping. Good grief, after all these years she should be immune to comments on her appearance. She started to lift another piece of lobster, but her fingers trembled. And Tom saw.

He stooped and took Annie's fingers in his. The perplexity on his face deepened.

'I've upset you, Annie. Why?'

'You haven't upset me.'

'Liar.'

'Tom. . .' Annie hauled her hand back from his. Tom released it, but he knelt on the cushions before her and watched her with eyes that were suddenly concerned.

'Annie, I haven't seen it before but. . . There's something wrong, isn't there? Something that makes you wear what you wear. Something that makes you wear your white coat and stethoscope as a shield. Or your awful T-shirts. Something that makes you afraid.'

'There's nothing wrong,' Annie said flatly. 'I like jeans and T-shirts, that's all. And as for something being wrong. . . It's you who has the problem. Remember?'

'But my small problem's sound asleep in her baby capsule.' Tom motioned to where Hannah slept soundly in the shade. 'My daughter's working up energy for tonight. So. . .now I can concentrate on you.'

'I don't see why you should do that all of a sudden,' Annie said crossly. Tom's interest was throwing her right off balance. 'I've been working here for eight months and you've never shown the least interest in me before.'

Tom's eyebrows snapped together.

'Yeah, well, maybe I've been remiss.'

'Or maybe you want something now.'

'I told you, Annie, I don't want anything.'

'Then why am I here?'

'Because dirty nappies scare the socks off me and she's due,' Tom said promptly—so promptly that Annie was forced to smile. Tom laughed with her, a deep chuckle that echoed out over the sand-hills around them.

Annie found herself smiling into Tom's eyes—and suddenly she found herself relaxing a fraction. Just a fraction, but it was enough. Maybe. . .maybe this could be fun. Maybe she could enjoy her picnic. She let Tom pour her champagne and then raised her brows in mock disapproval as he poured a glass for himself.

'OK, OK. I know I'm on call,' he told her, meeting

Annie's censorious look with laughter. 'But it's fine to have one glass. A glass of champagne just makes me feel intelligent.'

'More intelligent than you normally feel?' Annie teased. '*Wow*!' She smiled up at him, relaxing even more. It was hard to stay tense in such a place—on such a day—and she was far more comfortable when she could slip into the teasing banter she and Tom always used with each other. Brother and sister stuff. . .

Only she didn't feel like Tom McIver's sister.

Tom started talking about Robert Whykes's bad back and the problems he was having, coming to terms with long-term recuperation, and that helped. Immersed in her medicine, Annie could relax completely with this man—just savour his competence and caring. She put in her two bits' worth every now and then, but for the most part she was content to listen.

She lay back on her cushions, ate her lobster, sipped her champagne and tried as hard as she could to feel like Tom's kid sister. Or like a medical colleague and nothing else.

Impossible task! The champagne went straight to her head, and Annie started feeling weird. Nice—but weird.

This setting was magic. They were lying under gum trees on a bed of moss where the river rippled peacefully down to the sea. Fifty yards from where they lay the moss became sand and the sand sloped gently down to the beach. The faint wash of surf provided a sleepy background whisper. The dogs were chasing crazily after gulls—too far away to disturb them. Sunlight dappled through the leaves above their heads and Annie relaxed, ate, drank and let the peace of the day wash over her.

While Tom watched.

'You should go to sleep,' Annie told him, opening one eye to find him watching, and flushed under his gaze. 'I'll wake if the mobile phone rings, even if you don't. And you needn't worry. If you're called I'll wake you up fast enough. Considering how peaceful they are, I'll even let you leave Hannah and the dogs with me if you need to go back to the hospital. Just leave the left-over lobster when you go.'

'Generous to the bone!' Tom smiled but his smile was different. It was confused. As if he suddenly didn't know who he was with any more.

'Annie. . .'

'Hmm?' Annie was curled up on her mossy bed, her head on a mound of pillows. She'd drunk two glasses of champagne, her fingers were sleepily popping strawberries into her mouth and she was feeling indescribably happy.

Stupidly happy.

'Tell me about yourself.'

Annie considered while she ate more strawberries. It was a strange question—but, then, it was a strange day. A day out of the box.

'You know about me,' Annie said slowly, without opening her eyes. 'You read my résumé when I applied for the job.'

'I read your qualifications,' Tom told her. 'They're impressive. One of the youngest ever graduates from medical school. A year's rotational residency and then a year each of anaesthetics and paediatrics. Impeccable references from everyone. It was as if you were specifically training yourself for this job! But since you've been here. . .well, you don't seem interested in anything but medicine.'

'My medicine's important,' Annie told him. 'It's the most important thing in my life.'

'But. . . Annie, I do other things. Are you inferring my medicine's not important to me?'

Annie blinked—and then flushed.

'No, Tom,' she admitted, not meeting his look, 'I wasn't inferring you weren't dedicated. But. . . Yes, I'm committed to medicine. I thought that was what you wanted in a partner.'

'But you have room for outside interests, too—it's just that you don't want them.'

'That's right.' Annie shrugged, trying to shake off the memory of Tom's hurtful, overheard words: 'She'll work hard. If we're lucky, she'll grow to be a great old-maid doctor.' Tom McIver had employed her because she didn't seem to want outside interests. And now he was waiting to know why she didn't want them. 'I haven't been qualified long,' she managed. 'There's so much to learn.'

'With medicine, there's always so much to learn.' Tom poured coffee from a vacuum flask and handed her a mug. 'The trick is finding a balance.'

'Which you have?'

'Which I have,' Tom agreed. Then he glanced uncertainly across at the sleeping baby. 'The balance might just have to change now, though.'

Annie nodded. She drank her coffee and laid her empty mug carefully on the moss. As the champagne became diluted her dreamy haze cleared a bit. She thought through what he'd said, and moved the topic of conversation carefully away from herself.

'Tom, are you seriously thinking you might keep your baby?'

'Maybe.' Tom stared out at the beach to where his dogs were racing in crazy circles. They definitely were a sandwich short of a picnic, Annie thought. Dingbat dogs!

'Maybe meaning yes?'

Tom nodded.

'I'm starting to think so.' The laughter was gone from Tom's voice now. 'It's been a shock,' he said slowly, talking almost to himself. 'But I spoke to Melissa's mother on the phone this morning. Melissa arrived home from Israel eight and a half months pregnant, with the idea of having the baby adopted and then getting on with her life as fast as possible. The man she's currently fallen for is climbing mountains in Nepal and that's where Melissa wants to be. She doesn't give a toss about her baby. Our baby.'

He shrugged. 'So that leaves me—and I'll admit I'm finding it hard to be dispassionate. Objective. Maybe the best thing for Hannah is adoption. But...but I'm starting to think I want to keep her with me. I just can't bear not to. If only I could just figure out how.'

'Do you know anything about rearing children?' Annie asked, watching his face, and Tom grimaced.

'You know I don't. I don't know a damned thing, Annie, and that's the truth. But...' He shook his head and his eyes clouded. 'I know what it is not to be wanted. My parents never wanted me. My father tried to talk my mother into an abortion and she would have had one if she hadn't been afraid of the medical procedures.

'They made no bones about telling me I'd messed up their lives. I had teenage nannies until I was five and then my parents talked my grandmother into taking me. I hardly saw them after that. I was sent to boarding school soon after and, apart from my grandmother, I had nobody. The thought of my daughter being the same... The thought of her not being wanted...'

He closed his eyes and when he opened them again they were full of pain. 'I've been thinking and thinking,' he said harshly, 'and I don't think I can bear it. What Helen said last night. Not knowing who's looking after her. Not knowing what she's wearing—what she's doing. Knowing my daughter's alive in the world *and I'm not there.*'

His words were full of pain. Annie looked up at him. Tom's eyes were intense and brooding, as though he were looking back at a childhood full of rejection. And Annie's heart stirred in recognition.

'So...how about you, Annie?' Tom demanded, as if reading her thoughts. 'Did you play happy families all your childhood?'

'Who, me?' The switch of subject made Annie jump.

'Who else?'

Who else, indeed? Annie flushed and tried to make herself answer. She shouldn't mind the question. It was just. . .it was just that Tom's query was so personal— so exposing—and Annie wasn't used to people getting close.

But Tom had told her of his rejection. Told her about the loneliness of his childhood. And, by the look in his eyes, Annie knew he didn't confide often. She knew he'd spoken of something that still hurt.

And. . .maybe the only way to ease hurt was to share it. When sharing with Tom was something she'd wanted to do for so long. . .

'My dad walked out when I was tiny,' Annie admitted. 'And. . .my mum didn't want me either.' Annie shrugged. 'I have an older sister who's beautiful. My mum didn't know what to make of me.'

'But you're beautiful.'

It was a flippant remark. Stupid. He couldn't mean it. 'Tom, don't. . .'

'Did you spend all your childhood being told you were plain?' Tom asked incredulously, and the silence that greeted him was answer enough.

Annie flinched inside.

It sounded stupid now—that it had hurt so much. But Annie's mother was an ex-model who valued people solely on looks, and Annie's sister was long and willowy and. . .and just Tom's type.

When she was fifteen, a boy in senior school had asked Annie to go to a ball. He'd been a hunk, she remembered, and Annie had been astounded that she'd been chosen. She'd spent two months' clothing allowance on a dress she'd thought was fabulous.

Well, Annie's mother and sister had taken one look at Annie dressed up and had hooted in derision. And then the boy had come to collect her, and he'd met her sister. . .

End of story.

So Annie had given her dress to charity, put on her jeans and baggy T-shirts and told herself she was made for working. The boys she'd dated after that had been those who'd lived and breathed study and work.

Until she'd met Tom, that is. Since Tom, somehow she'd had trouble dating anyone. And how stupid was that?

'You hide all your lights,' Tom said gently, and by his voice Annie could tell he'd seen unhappiness wash over her. 'Annie. . .'

'Tom, don't. . .'

Annie put her hand up to prevent him—but not fast enough. Tom's fingers reached out and lifted her glasses from her nose. And laid them aside on the rug. Before she could realize what he was about, his skilful fingers found the clip at the back of her hair—and lifted it to let her curls fall free.

And then he sat back and looked at her as her soft curls tumbled down about her shoulders.

'Don't ever let anyone tell you you're not beautiful, Annie Burrows,' Tom said gently. 'Don't ever believe them. If they say that then they're liars.'

That was a bit much! 'Tom McIver, how can you say that? When for the last eight months you haven't so much as looked at me. . .'

'I haven't looked past your defences until now,' Tom said softly. 'And maybe I've been a fool.' He raised his hand and pushed a wispy curl back behind her ear—and Annie flinched as if she'd been burned.

'What's wrong?' Tom asked.

'I don't like—'

'You don't like me touching you?'

He had to be kidding! All Annie wanted him to do was touch her. But she still didn't trust him. She was here as a Sarah substitute, she thought desperately. A fall-back position because Sarah had let him down.

Hold onto that thought.

'Tom. . .it's time to go.'

'It's not time for us to go,' Tom said firmly. 'Rob will call us if he needs us. Murray's asthma is subsiding. Mr Stotter's angina has settled. Rod Manning will be sleeping off his hangover. We can't set his arm until his alcohol level is right down and all he'll do if we come near is abuse us. There's nothing else that needs doing. It's Sunday afternoon and Bannockburn's asleep.'

'Then we should be sleeping too,' Annie muttered. 'Tom. . .what if we're up again tonight?'

'Then we'll worry about that tonight. Annie, why are you afraid?'

'I'm not afraid.'

'You mean. . .' Tom stirred on the cushions and moved closer to look directly into her frightened eyes. 'You mean, if I kiss you, you won't flinch?'

'You don't. . .you don't want to kiss me.'

'Yes, I do.'

'Tom. . .'

But Tom wasn't listening. His hand had come out and caught the back of her head and pulled her face forward—forward so that his lips could meet hers in a first gentle kiss of exploration. And it was done so suddenly that there was nothing Annie could do to prevent it.

If she'd wanted to.

So Tom kissed her. And it was the kiss that Annie had dreamed of all her life.

It was a kiss of questions. A kiss of wonder. A kiss that held a faint astonishment on Tom's part that he'd wanted to do such a thing. He'd never thought of Annie Burrows as a woman before. And yet. . . And yet here she was before him, and her face was soft and her eyes were huge and wondering. . .

And when his mouth met hers the kiss slammed home the knowledge that Annie was every inch a woman. As desirable as any Melissa. . .or Sarah. . . Or any other woman. . . As desirable, or more desirable. . .

Because, as their lips met, it was like two halves of
a whole fitting together—two pieces of a shattered coin
being joined again after years apart. Each slot and niche
and fold fitted into itself with a certainty that couldn't
be argued with.

Tom's body stiffened in shocked recognition. His
mind stilled as his mouth tasted the girl he was holding.

Quite suddenly, nothing in his life had ever felt so
good before—or so right.

And Annie. . .

For a moment Annie's mouth didn't move beneath
his. She didn't respond at all. And then, as though
moved by a force stronger than self-control—stronger
than anything she'd ever known—Tom felt a desire to
respond overwhelm her. He felt her lips move softly
beneath his—then part—and open themselves to him
as a flower welcomes summer rain.

As a woman welcomes her man home.

Dear God. . . Something was happening here that was
stronger than both of them.

Tom's hands fell to pull Annie's body against his—
to feel her soft curves yield so that her breasts pressed
against his chest. His kiss deepened, as did the wonder.
His mouth devoured hers, tasting her—finding her inner
being and wanting more. . . Wanting to know what this
wonder could be that he was finding in such an unexpec-
ted corner of his life.

This woman under his hands was like no woman he'd
ever thought he'd wanted.

Annie wore no make-up. She looked up at him with
eyes that held no hint of the coquette. Annie had been
a colleague and a friend for eight months and secretly,
in her inner being, she'd held this wonder—the capacity
to make his soul ache with a need that was almost
overwhelming. It was a need that he'd never known
he had.

And, in his shock, it was Tom who withdrew—who

pulled back and gazed at the girl before him with eyes that were dark with passion and with shock.

'Annie. . .' Tom's voice was a husky whisper.

'No!'

For a long, long moment they stared at each other in stunned silence, and then somehow Annie managed to pull away—to rise from Tom's cushions and his pillows and to haul herself out of his dangerous range.

'What. . .what do you think you're doing?' she faltered, white-faced and trembling. 'Tom. . . How dare you. . .?'

'Annie. . .' Tom made to rise but Annie took two more hasty steps away.

'No.'

'Annie, it was only a kiss. . .'

'I know.' She couldn't keep her voice from shaking. 'That's all. A kiss. . .'

Nothing, she told herself savagely. A kiss meant nothing!

'You toad. . . You toad. . .'

'You wanted to be kissed as much as I wanted to kiss you,' Tom said mildly, watching her face. 'It's not such a crime.'

'It is!'

'You're not telling me you've reached twenty-five without being kissed!'

'No! No! But it means more to me. . .'

Annie was practically in tears. How could she explain to this man that his kiss—this one kiss that meant so little to Tom McIver—had transformed her life?

Before this moment she'd known she was in love with Tom, but she'd also known that such a love was crazy and senseless and she could live her life here, knowing she was being stupid.

But how could she go on now?

Tom stood motionless, watching her across the clearing. Annie had all the signs of a frightened deer, ready to bolt for cover. 'Annie, I'm sorry—but I wanted to kiss you badly,' he said softly.

'Well, I don't know why you should,' she managed, and there was even a trace of crossness in her voice. 'Unless it's just because I'm female.'

'Meaning I'll go after anything in a skirt.'

'*Yes!*'

Tell it like it is!

'I see.' And, damn him, the laughter was flooding back into Tom's eyes.

'It's true, isn't it?' Annie felt confusion give way to anger. How dared he make her feel like this—how dared he! 'How many women have you gone out with in the valley since I've been here?' she demanded. 'I must be pretty much the only one you haven't asked. Does that pique your pride, Tom McIver? One woman left untouched. . . Is that why you're trying to make love to me?'

'It's not true.' Tom was almost as off balance as Annie. Despite the laughter, there was still confusion in his eyes.

'I'm no scalp to be added to your belt.'

Tom rose and took two long strides off the rug to where Annie was standing. Strong hands caught her shoulders and held her. He looked down into her face long and hard, searching behind the defiance.

And what he saw there made him draw in his breath.

'Annie, you're no scalp,' he told her strongly. 'Don't ever think I'd do that to you, Annie. Don't!'

'But. . .'

'You're afraid.'

'I'm not! Why should I be afraid?'

'I won't hurt you, Annie.'

'I know you won't hurt me,' Annie snapped, trying desperately to haul herself free. 'You won't hurt me because I won't let myself be hurt. Last night you kissed Sarah. Now you kiss me. And you say I'm not another scalp!'

'You're different from Sarah.'

'I'm different to the lot of them,' Annie said harshly. 'You don't want me, Tom McIver. You're just filling in time until the next Sarah flies into your orbit. Or the next Melissa. Or whoever. . .'

And then, at the sound of a tiny whimper behind her, Annie gave a sob of relief. She hauled herself away from him and reached into the baby capsule to retrieve his daughter. She lifted Hannah into her arms and held the little girl before her defensively.

'Tom, stop playing games,' she said, and her words were pleading. Her wide eyes looked up at Tom and her words tumbled out too fast. 'You must. . .you must get your life in order. Going from woman to woman. . . Living the life you do. . . Tom, you have to stop. . .stop this. . .play-acting. . .if you're serious about giving this little one a home. . .'

Tom's eyes were dark and fathomless. 'It's not play-acting, Annie. And I *am* serious.'

'Really?'

'Really.'

Silence.

And Tom stood motionless, staring at the girl before him. Annie stood, slight and confused, with her bare toes curled into the moss and her arms holding his daughter against her breast. Woman and child. . . Tom took one more step forward—and then he stopped, stunned.

He looked like someone who'd been hit by a vision. Or a lightning bolt.

Annie tightened her hold on Hannah. Reassured by Annie's arms that adults were present and her food supply hadn't been cut off, the baby ceased her whimpering, nestled happily in Annie's arms and cooed. While Annie stared up at Tom in bewilderment.

'Tom, what is it?'

'I've just had a thought,' Tom said blankly. 'It's. . . Annie, it's. . .'

'What thought?' Annie said impatiently—exasperated. 'Tom. . .'

'It's something Helen said to me before she went off duty this morning. I thought she was crazy, but now. . . Annie, she was right and I think I must have been crazy not to see it. She was right all the time.'

'What. . .'

'Annie, will you marry me?'

CHAPTER SIX

ANNIE gaped. And gaped some more.

Then Tom finally recovered some of his equilibrium. After all, he'd had two whole minutes longer than Annie to get used to the idea.

'Close your mouth, Annie,' Tom said at last, his ridiculous laughter surfacing again. 'You'll catch flies.'

'Tell me what you just said,' Annie managed faintly, and Tom smiled.

Of course he smiled. The man treated life as a permanent joke. Only this joke was sick. Cruel. But. . . Tom didn't sound as if he was joking. Only the words he was saying weren't making sense.

'I'm asking you to marry me, Annie,' Tom said gently, still smiling. 'There's no need to look so dumbfounded.'

Annie took a ragged breath—and steadied herself.

'Oh, of course,' she muttered, gathering strength as well as indignation. Some joke! 'Of course,' she repeated, her anger growing. 'No need at all to look surprised! Good grief, Tom McIver! On Friday night Melissa hands over *your* baby. Saturday night you tell me you're marrying Sarah. And now. . . Now you kiss *me* and ask me to marry you. Totally logical, really! Why didn't I expect it? It's a wonder I didn't rush out this morning to buy a wedding dress.' She lifted her eyes to his, and her eyes flashed with fury.

'Do you have an engagement ring for me, Tom?' she demanded. 'And is it my size? Or is it Sarah's? Or Melissa's? Or does it fit someone I haven't even heard of yet? Tomorrow's lover.'

'Annie. . .'

'Don't mess me around, Tom,' she snapped. 'You

91

can make sick jokes with all your other damned women—but not with me. I thought I was a doormat—but now I see that it's all your other women who are the doormats. You use women, Tom McIver, *and you're not using me.*'

'I don't. . .'

But Annie was no longer listening. 'I'm walking home,' she snapped. 'You can just stay here and try and think of some other lover you can add to your stupid list. Some other doormat.'

And before Tom had a chance to reply she whirled round and hiked off as fast as her legs could carry her—over the sand hills to the beach beyond.

She would have headed for the road, but Tom was in her path to the road and there was a way home along the beach.

Annie forgot one thing.

She forgot she was carrying a baby. Tom's baby. Fifty yards across the sand hills, when she suddenly realized Hannah was still in her arms, it seemed impossible to turn, to go back and hand over Hannah. By that time Tom was already moving after her.

To run while carrying a baby in her arms was well night impossible. If Annie had stomped off any faster over the soft sand she would have tripped and fallen. Even so, by the time Tom caught her—by the simple expedient of moving quickly past her and then turning to block her path—Annie was out of breath and out of places to run.

She'd headed straight for the sea. Now she stood just where the waves reached in their incoming rush, and the wet sand oozed up through her bare toes. Baulked, she stood still and glared as Tom placed his hands on her shoulders. And in her arms Hannah gurgled her delight at all this action.

'Can I have my daughter back?' Tom said mildly, and Annie glared some more.

'You don't deserve her, you womanizing toad. . .'

'I'm not a womanizer.'

'Oh, no?'

'Look, Annie, I don't sleep with every woman I go out with!' Tom sounded exasperated.

'How very discriminating!' Annie was almost past speaking. Fury was threatening to choke her.

And, in her arms, Hannah chuckled.

Tom gave his daughter a sideways grin—and then focused on Annie again, as if politely assuring her of the importance of what she was saying.

Patronizing. . .arrogant. . .

'Annie, it may come as a surprise to you, but you're the very first woman I've ever proposed to.'

'Oh, really? How very kind of you! And I'm supposed to go down on bended knee with gratitude?'

'Well, a bit of common courtesy might be nice,' Tom said bluntly. 'I don't see what I've done to have you react with anger. Honestly, Annie, think about it. Helen said if I was serious about finding a wife I should look no further than you. I thought she was crazy and then, when I kissed you, I suddenly saw she was right. It would be sensible.'

'Sensible?' Annie's voice was rising fast to a squeak. 'What could be sensible about marrying you?'

Tom gave his daughter another grin, and then transferred his smile to Annie. 'Annie, we could be a family. The three of us.'

'Oh, yeah?' Annie managed in between angry gasps. 'Three? There aren't just three, though, are there, Tom McIver? There's a whole menagerie. Me and you and Hannah, and your two idiot dogs—and every other unattached woman in this town. And probably even a few attached ones as well.'

Tom sighed. 'Annie, I am *not* a womanizer!'

'So you keep saying. Pull the other leg. It plays *Jingle Bells*.'

'Annie. . .'

'I'm going home!'

'Would you like to give me my daughter back first?'
Tom asked mildly. 'You know possession's nine tenths
of the law. If you keep her she's yours.'

Annie glared. 'You'd like that, wouldn't you?' Annie
said bitterly. 'A nice convenient mother for your child.
Knock a hole between our two apartments and push
Hannah through to me whenever you're entertaining
one of your—'

'Annie, I am offering you a serious marriage proposal.' Tom's smile faded as his voice rose in
exasperation. He lifted his daughter from her arms and
then glared straight back at Annie, anger meeting anger.
'I'm serious, Annie. I do mean it when I say we could
be a family. And families mean faithfulness.'

'Oh, sure,' Annie jeered. 'You'd be faithful to me—
as payment—while I care for you and your daughter
and your two dogs.' She paused as the sound of the
dogs' barking reached a crescendo, the noise momentarily—blessedly—distracting her. 'And if you don't
stop your dogs chasing birds, Dr McIver, I'll report you
to the RSPCA. They're killing something.'

'The birds are enjoying their exercise,' Tom retorted.
'If you think any bird stands in danger of being caught
then you don't know Tiny and Hoof. Look, Annie. . .'

But Annie was no longer listening. She'd turned
blindly to watch the birds—to see anything but Tom
McIver's face—and she hadn't seen any birds. What
she saw. . .

'Tom!'

Tom stopped in mid-sentence at the sudden urgency
in Annie's voice. Annie was staring along the beach
where the dogs were barking themselves frantic. Instead
of their bird-chasing, though, the dogs had transferred
their attention to something along the beach where the
river met the sea.

'Tom, they're not chasing birds,' Annie said urgently,
her own attention changing direction as swiftly as the
dogs' had done. 'Tom, there's a boat in trouble!'

'A boat. . .' Tom stared blankly up the beach. 'Annie. . .'

'I saw it,' Annie said faintly. 'Upside down in the river mouth. The waves are washing over it. It's under now but watch!'

Hannah was unceremoniously thrust back into Annie's arms as Tom swivelled round. 'I can't see. . .'

'It's under water now. Tom. . .I think I saw someone. . .just for a minute. . . But I think he was washed off when it went under.'

But Tom was no longer beside her. He was already running up the beach.

So, what *did* one do in an emergency when one was left holding the baby?

Annie stared down at Hannah's tiny face while her mind clicked into gear. OK. First things first. Call for help and find somewhere safe to put Hannah.

Then, forgetting to fret about stumbling, she ran almost as fast as Tom, but in the direction of the car and mobile phone. One fast phone call to the ambulance.

'Dave, a boat's hit rocks at the river entrance. It's upside down and someone's in trouble. I don't know any more.'

'I'll contact the lifeboat crew and be with you in five minutes,' Dave growled and shoved the phone down.

Done. What next?

Dear God, don't let Tom try to rescue someone on his own. . .

Annie grabbed the emergency bag from Tom's luggage compartment. What else? A rope. . .if there was one. . . Blessedly, there was. A coil of rope lay with Tom's car tools. Annie looped it round her neck, put Hannah back in her baby capsule and set off again at a run, capsule at one side and medical bag at the other.

The bag and baby capsule combined weighed a ton. At the end of this Annie's arms might have been stretched six inches longer, but now her burden hardly slowed her at all.

Hannah must wonder just what sort of crazy life she'd tumbled into, Annie thought wryly as the baby jogged up and down at Annie's side. She lay back in her baby capsule and gurgled and watched and enjoyed every minute of this new experience. She was some baby! She was Tom's daughter in every way.

There was a rocky outcrop where the river met the sea, a bank of sorts, providing a sheltered entrance at low tide. But it was high tide now and the water was crashing over the edge. From where they'd stood on the beach Annie had been able to see over it, but closer she couldn't.

'OK, Hannah, you're on your own,' she muttered as she reached the rocks, the thought of Tom fighting his way through the water on the other side of the bank making her priorities easy. Hannah would be safe enough—much safer than Tom!

Tom's two great dogs were standing on the bank. Their barking had stopped and they were wearing identical expressions of dog-like concern. They looked as fearful as Annie felt.

So. . .

So Annie placed Hannah above the high-water mark on the sand, checked that the baby was facing away from the sun and then clambered up the bank to see. And drew in her breath in horror.

The boat was almost submerged. Whoever was in charge of the boat had headed in when the water had been too high to make the entrance safe. Annie had been warned of this place when she'd first moved here.

'The entrance is safe when the water's low across the rocks, but as soon as the rocks are submerged there are all sorts of currents and cross-waves that'll crash a boat into the wall. If you go out at low tide, make sure you get back in before the water rises.'

Annie had never been tempted to try, but this time. . .

Whoever was in the boat had tried and failed. The boat had smashed into the rocks. Annie could see a mass of shattered wood that was the sinking hull, but the man Annie had thought she'd seen was nowhere in sight.

Tom was. Just.

He was swimming strongly across the current, and Annie caught her breath in fear at the sight of him. Tom was a strong swimmer but the waves were breaking over the rocks, sending spray over the ledge Annie had climbed, and the sea inside the river mouth was a maelstrom of white water.

He couldn't make it. . .

Dear God. . .

There was nothing she could do. Annie stood uselessly on the bank, clutching the doctor's bag like a talisman, watching. She never took her eyes from Tom.

He reached the upturned hull. There were waves hitting it from both sides. The man must have been an idiot to try and come through. In these conditions, the only safe thing to do was to wait for low tide. He couldn't have known. . . And now he was putting Tom at risk.

Annie allowed herself a fierce glance around, willing the surf lifeboat to appear from the ocean or the ambulance from the landside. Of course it was too soon. There was nothing—only Tom. And then Tom disappeared, diving under the hull.

The world stopped. Ten seconds. Twenty. Thirty. . .

Annie was counting in her head. Thirty-two. . . Thirty-three. . . How long could he hold his breath?

And then Tom's head broke the surface, and in his grasp he had what he'd been searching for. The body of a man. . .

Annie dumped the bag on the ledge, wedging it so that it couldn't be swept away, and scrambled down to where the waves broke over her. She went as far as she dared into the water, keeping a fierce toe-hold on her rocks. Before Tom could drag the man anywhere near her she was looping her rope and spreading her hands, trying to work out when she could reasonably throw it.

The currents were swirling round in shifting patterns. It was past high tide now and the bulk of the water was moving out to sea. Tom swam on his side, concentrating fiercely on keeping the man's head out of water. He was making no headway at all—and he was being slowly swept out to sea.

Now! Her brain screamed the word at her, even though she knew she could hardly reach him. But if she didn't throw it now. . .

Annie wedged the end of the rope under her foot, eighteen inches under water. Then, holding the loop as wide and high as she could, Annie threw with every ounce of strength she possessed.

It landed four feet short.

Sobbing in terror, Annie hauled the rope back in, but Tom had seen what she was doing. He looked fleetingly back at her—and then Annie knew he was kicking himself toward her with superhuman strength.

He couldn't make it. It was up to her.

She looped—and threw.

Tom let one hand loose from his burden, grabbed—and held.

Annie hauled for her life—and two minutes later Tom was scrambling up the rocks, with Annie helping him drag his lifeless burden after him.

'Mask. . .' Exhausted beyond belief, Tom was hardly able to speak as he dragged himself out of the water. 'I've got him. We can't. . . Oh, God, get the mask, Annie. . .'

Annie was already moving, fighting her way out of the water to reach the bag.

It was a dreadful place to try resuscitation. On dry sand it would have been difficult enough, but there was no time to carry him to the beach. Instead, Tom and Annie used their bodies to block the wash of water as they fought desperately to find some response.

'Breathe, damn you. Breathe.' Tom pumped rhythmically on the man's chest as Annie worked the mask. Tirelessly they worked, knowing the man had a chance. If Annie had seen him above the surface then he couldn't have been under water for more than five minutes.

Breathe. . . And finally he did—a raw, choking splutter that turned into a vomit of sea water. And another.

And then the man's eyes opened and he looked up in a haze of bewilderment.

'Wh—' He couldn't speak. The word spluttered into a cough and he fell back.

'You're safe. Take it easy.' Tom held the man's head slightly raised. There was still urgency in his voice, though. He'd thought what Annie hadn't dared to think. 'But tell us whether there was anyone else on board. Was there anyone with you? We need to know *now*!'

Silence.

Annie was scarcely breathing herself.

Blessedly, the man shook his head.

Dear God. . .

And then, suddenly, there were people everywhere. Dave and his partner were racing across the sand with oxygen and a stretcher, and out to sea the lifeboat appeared around the headland, with its captain shouting through a megaphone.

Annie squatted back and felt like bursting into tears.

'Don't do it, Dr Burrows,' Tom said gently before they all arrived. 'It'll destroy your reputation as a dour lady doctor.' He reached out and touched her gently on the face. 'And your hair is still hanging free and you're minus glasses and you've just saved my life. . . And you look. . .you look. . .' He broke off, but not before Annie heard the raw emotion in his voice.

She didn't deserve what he was saying.

'I did not save your life,' she whispered. 'You did it yourself. . .'

'We would have been swept out onto the rocks on

the reef. . .' Tom shook his head and then smiled down at the man, still struggling to catch his breath. 'Take your time, mate. Thanks to this lady, you have all the time in the world.'

'Thanks to you both. . .' The man choked, gasped and fell silent.

After that, there was little more for Annie to do.

The lifeboat went disconsolately home, the boys irked that it wasn't them who'd done the rescuing, and the ambulancemen loaded their patient onto a stretcher. Tom set up an oxygen mask over the man's face, trying to get some colour back into him.

There was now no trace of the boat.

'I'll go back with the ambulance,' Tom told Annie quietly. 'He's still not breathing well and I'm not sure it's just shock. I need to check his lungs.' He hesitated. 'Can you bring the car back?'

Annie managed a smile. 'I guess. . . If you don't mind a soggy backside on your driver's seat.'

'You can put your soggy backside anywhere you please.' Tom smiled at her in a way that made Annie's heart do a back flip. 'Thank you, Annie. That's the best lassoing job I've ever seen. It seems a bit rough now to land you with my daughter and dogs.'

'I don't mind. Only this once.'

'Mmm.' Tom checked the mask again and then turned to give Annie one last smile.

'OK, that's it. Go and find yourself some dry clothes. We'll continue our picnic at some later date.'

'Tom. . .'

'Don't think I'm letting my really good idea rest in peace, Annie,' he told her, and his voice was dead serious. He put a hand up and pushed his sodden hair back from his eyes. 'The more I think of it the more I like it, Annie Burrows. All you have to learn is how sensible it is.'

Annie sighed and turned away. 'Don't! Tom, your

proposal. . .your proposal is about as sensible as your two dogs!'

'And my two dogs just found a man who would have drowned if he hadn't been seen,' Tom said, and his tone was dead serious. 'Sense is where you find it, Annie. Think about it.' His smile deepened. 'And, by the way, look at my dogs now.' He motioned to the beach where Annie had dumped the baby capsule.

Hannah was in good hands. The dogs had taken themselves back to where the baby lay and they stood like two stern sentinels, one on either side of the capsule.

'She's ours,' their body language said. 'We're on guard. Touch her if you dare!'

'As sensible as my two dogs?' Tom reached out and gripped Annie's hand in a gesture that was hardly more than a fleeting touch—but was as intimate as any caress. 'I happen to think that my dogs are very, very sensible. And so is my proposal.'

Hannah was taken out of Annie's care as soon as she reached the hospital. Mrs Farley, the hospital cook, fussed out as soon as she arrived back.

'You go and change, dear. The ambulance is here and we know all about it. You must be exhausted. I'll look after this one. She's such a little pet—and, by the way, I've had a really good idea about who else would love to help look after her.'

So Annie showered and changed—and then tried to figure what to do with the rest of her afternoon.

Tom didn't need her.

Albert Hopper, the boatman, was recovering. His lungs were clear enough. Rob had told her when she rang the nurses' station so Annie was free to avoid Tom as much as she liked.

It wasn't easy. The hospital was too small.

She tried to work but no one needed her. The little hospital was quiet. The only patient not asleep or knee-deep in visitors was Rod Manning, who abused her so thoroughly when she approached that she retired in haste.

'You gave that sample to the cops, you bloody bitch. Do you know what that'll cost me? You had no right. I'll sue! Just let me get out of here and get to my lawyers. And why can't you give me anything else for the pain. . .?'

Annie couldn't defend herself in the face of his fury. She boosted his painkillers as high as she dared and took herself out of range of his invective.

She tried doing paperwork in her office—but she could hear Tom moving about the little hospital. She could hear his voice giving orders, and he and Robbie laughing at a joke she couldn't hear. She couldn't work at all.

Finally she shoved her beeper on so she could be contacted in an emergency and took a sheaf of paperwork out under the gums at the back of the hospital. She found a spot where no one could find her—and settled down to dictate letters.

She couldn't stay there for ever.

She went for a long walk at dusk, and came back well after dark. Then she had to listen to Tom all over again. She heard him give Hannah her late feed. She heard the baby fuss and then settle.

After ten minutes of holding her breath there was a knock on her door which she didn't feel like answering.

What she needed here was a bit of resolution.

'Go away, Tom. It's late, I'm tired and I don't want to see you.'

Her voice echoed from the walls and Annie winced as she listened to herself. Her words sounded petty.

'Why not?' Tom's voice was bland—smooth as milk. 'Are you afraid? Is your hair still down?'

'No!' Annie snatched up her glasses and shoved them hard on her nose. Shield up! Her defences still felt fragile.

'Annie, let me in.'

'I'm too tired.'

'And I'm too tired to talk through a closed door. If I yell any louder I'll wake up patients. Come on, Annie. I need to talk.'

'What about?'

'Medicine.' Tom's voice assumed a note of pious duty. 'Annie, it's your professional duty to open the door.'

'Very subtle!' Annie glared at the closed door. 'I'll bet the big bad wolf never tried that line at the pigs' house. Why don't you just huff and puff, blow yourself out and then go away?'

'Annie, this is stupid. We need to talk.' Tom sighed heavily on the other side of the door. 'Don't you think you're being just a tiny bit paranoid?'

Annie glared some more.

'Annie?'

OK. OK. She knew she was being petty. Or just too scared for words.

Taking a deep breath, she swung the door wide and Annie's personal wolf grinned in triumph—and marched right in.

Straight through to her kitchen.

'Where do you think you're going?'

Annie stood by the door and glared. Tom was considerably dryer than the last time she'd seen him. He was wearing his white coat over clean trousers, his stethoscope swung from his neck at a crazy angle and his curls didn't look like they'd been combed after his shower. And one look at him was enough to make Annie's heart do back flips.

She had an almost irresistible urge to straighten his stethoscope—and comb his hair. Or just touch it!

'I'm making coffee,' Tom told her, ignoring her hostility. 'God knows, I need it.'

'Why don't you make coffee next door?' For some reason it was hard to make her voice work.

'Because my sink is full of bottles that need sterilizing and pans from making formula. I need a housekeeper.'

'Yeah, so you said.' Annie was talking to his back as he filled her plunger with coffee grounds and ran water into her kettle. 'And I'm supposed to be it.'

Tom swung around from the kettle and his face stilled.

'Annie, I didn't ask you to be my housekeeper,' he said gently, meeting her gaze with calmness and honesty. 'I asked you to be my wife.'

'So what's the difference?' Annie's voice was bitter, but that was the way she was feeling. Bitter as all heck! It was all very well for this man to throw marriage proposals in her direction. It didn't turn *his* life upside down.

'Hey, Annie. . .' In a few swift strides Tom crossed back to where she still held the door open. He seized her arms and hauled her close against his chest. Behind her, the door closed with a thump. 'Annie, that's a crazy question.'

Annie held herself still. The feel of Tom's chest against her breasts was making her heart thump. Somehow, though, she had to make herself say it.

'You. . .you mean you want me for sex as well as housework?'

Silence.

Carefully Tom let go his grip on her. He stood for a long, silent moment, staring down at her troubled face, and then he turned and went back to his coffee.

'Let's start this again, shall we?' he said politely, concentrating on the coffee. 'Can I make you a drink?'

'I don't want one. I want to go to bed.' Annie was being as rude as she could, but she didn't seem to have a choice. Her heart felt as if it were shrivelling inside. Tom was offering her something she'd dreamed of for years, and she was thrusting it away as worthless.

No. It wasn't true.

Tom wasn't offering her her dream. Tom was offering her marriage. And what Annie wanted—all Annie wanted—was Tom's love. One without the other didn't make sense at all.

So now she did what she'd always done in times of distress. Retired into her work.

'How's Albert?' she asked, and crossed the room to sit on a kitchen chair. The chair was hard and she sat stiffly upright. Her body felt as if it were about to snap.

'He's not good.' Tom's face snapped down in a frown, following her lead back into medicine as he carried his coffee to the table.

'His lungs are clear enough, and he'll recover from shock, but his ego's taken such a dent it'll take a while to mend. If it ever does. He's fished that entrance so many times he reckons he knows it like the back of his hand. His wife came to see me tonight and says he can hardly speak to her. . . Can hardly look at her. . . And his boat wasn't insured.'

'Oh, no. . .'

Tom shrugged. 'Albert's lectured local kids time and time again on the danger of the bar. The fact that he broke the rules—and nearly lost his life, doing it—will take some living down.' He met her eyes and managed a smile. 'Familiarity breeds contempt, they say. Maybe it's true. Like me and you, Annie. I was so familiar with you I never saw what was before my eyes.'

'Tom, don't.' Annie flinched and stared at her hands. She stayed silent while Tom drank his coffee—and while he quietly watched her.

'Shouldn't you be getting back to Hannah?' she murmured as he set down his empty mug.

'She's just through this wall, and I can hear every whimper. It's no different to being in the next room. Now, if we knocked a door between us. . .'

'No!'

'Annie, why the hell not?'

'Tom, I won't go knocking holes in walls—and I won't be getting married just because you need a babysitter.' Annie's breath was coming in painful gasps. 'I won't. And, besides. . .'

'Besides?'

'I don't know whether you've considered, but marrying me wouldn't solve your problems. In an emergency we're both needed. You're much better off marrying someone like Sarah.'

'I don't want to marry Sarah.'

'Well, keep looking for someone else.'

'I don't want to keep looking either,' Tom said softly, watching Annie so steadily that colour started sweeping across her face. 'Unless it's at you. I've decided you have the cutest nose of anyone I know.'

'You're not telling me you've fallen in love with me since this afternoon?' Annie's words were practically a jeer. Her whole consciousness was twisting in pain.

'Well, no. . .'

'There you go, then.' Annie stood up so fast that she jolted the table and made Tom's mug slip sideways. 'End of story.'

'Are you saying you'll only marry if you fall in love?' Tom stayed exactly where he was, his voice calmly meditative. His calmness made Annie's pain worse.

But somehow she made her voice stay calm to match his. 'Tom, I doubt if I'll ever marry.' The pain of Tom's words in her first week at Bannockburn swept over her in bitter memory. 'And I thought. . .I thought an old-maid doctor was what you wanted here.'

'Who told you that?' Tom's face had stilled.

'I heard it,' Annie said bitterly. 'I heard you say it the first week I was here. That's what you wanted— but now you think I might be more useful as something else. A little domestic appendage. . .'

'Annie, stop this!' Tom rose, kicked his chair out of the way and came round to Annie's side of the table. Her white face told him exactly how distressed she was.

'Hell, Annie, I might have said that once—but I didn't mean to hurt you. . .'

'Well, you have.' Annie's voice was a jagged whisper.

'Then I'm sorry, but let's leave it.' Tom reached out to hold her again, his hands gripping her shoulders and his head tilting so he could look into her pain-filled eyes. 'Let's leave it as something I might have thought before I knew you. Annie, don't look so upset. I'm not asking you to marry me tomorrow.' The irrepressible grin burst out. 'Next Saturday's fine. That's six whole days to sort yourself out.'

'Tom. . .'

'I know. I know.' His smile became placating, affectionate, intimate. 'I'm pushing. In fact, there's a four-week waiting period before we can legally do it. But it does seem like a great idea, Annie.'

'Great for whom?' Annie made a huge effort to make her voice work properly. She glared up at Tom and found his eyes inches from hers. Too close by half. 'What's in it for me, Tom?' she managed. 'You stand to gain a babysitter and a dogsitter and a domestic convenience. What do I stand to gain?'

'Well, I beat a hot-water bottle!'

It was said so fast—so blatantly—that Annie gave a startled jolt within Tom's hold—and stared. Despite her confusion, the sides of her mouth curved into laughter.

Toad!

'I prefer a hot-water bottle that doesn't take half the bed.' Somehow Annie fought her insidious laughter back and she shook her head. 'No, Tom. The idea's crazy.'

'It's not crazy, Annie. Think about it.' He stood back from her, but his eyes didn't leave her face. 'Annie, we've both come from backgrounds where we've learned that romantic love is for the birds. Your dad walked out and my parents were dysfunctional, to say the least. We've had a rough deal with our families.

'Maybe. . .maybe a marriage that's based on common sense and friendship might be ideal. And I know we could be good together. I felt that in one short kiss. And you felt it, too. We pack a powerful punch, Annie Burrows, and we could have a very satisfying long-term partnership.'

They could. Or, rather, he could.

Romantic love is for the birds. . .

Tom's hands were holding hers now, making her feel wanted and cherished and all the things she could never be.

Solid, sensible Annie. . .

How would Tom McIver cope with such a marriage when he realized his wife was absolutely, totally in love with him? Annie wondered dully. She was so in love that if Tom treated her as a useful friend and nothing more it would tear her heart in two.

Oh, God, why did it have to be so hard?

Why couldn't she just say, 'Yes, I'll marry you.'

Because. . .because she wanted such an announcement to be met with joy. With a love and commitment to match her own.

If she said it now—said, 'Yes, I'll marry you'— Tom would just as likely give her a perfunctory kiss of satisfaction and take himself to bed. To *his* bed. On *his* side of the wall.

Bargain sealed. A nice satisfactory contract. He'd have found a steady, sensible mother for his daughter.

Well, Annie wasn't it!

'I'm not marrying you, Tom,' Annie told him, and only she knew the pain her words were causing within her heart. 'I'm not marrying anyone.'

And she knew what else she had to say.

'And I can't stay here,' she added, and she watched as Tom's eyes widened. 'Not now. Not. . .not with this between us. I'll stay until you have the chance to find another doctor for the town. But consider that I've handed in my notice.'

'I'm leaving, Tom. I wish you the best of luck with your daughter. With your life. But. . .but I don't have any part in it.'

HARLEQUIN ROMANCE   159

'I'm leaving, Tom. I wish you the best of luck with
your daughter. With work like Doll's, Ian, I don't have
any part in it.'

CHAPTER SEVEN

SOMEHOW Annie got some sleep that night—but not
very much. She woke, feeling as if she'd been run over
by a train, and her face, when she worked up enough
courage to look in the mirror, told her much the same.

Her mother and sister would have too much sense to
cry themselves to sleep, she told herself crossly.
Showered and dressed, she made a dive out to the dis-
pensary to find eye-drops. They made her eyes feel
better but they didn't reduce the swelling.

'So. . .it's clinic in dark glasses this morning,' she
muttered, and headed out to face the world through
green-tinted frames.

'Dr Burrows, why are you wearing sunglasses
inside?' The first nurse she saw asked the question when
Annie wasn't two feet inside the hospital corridor. She
muttered something about hayfever and felt like bolting
for cover.

It was worse when Robbie saw her. The nursing
administrator checked out Annie's glasses and said
nothing at all.

'I have hayfever,' Annie said defiantly. Robbie just
nodded.

And pigs fly, his look said.

Then Tom came out of a side ward and the urge to
bolt became almost overwhelming but, mercifully, Tom
was acting as though nothing at all was between them.

'Dr Burrows, we need to set Rod Manning's arm this
morning,' Tom said briefly, ignoring her glasses. 'The
sooner we get the thing set and get him out of here the
happier I'll be.'

'You mean he's still furious?'

'His temper hasn't subsided with his alcohol level.'

110

Tom grimaced with distaste. 'I've been in touch with Melbourne this morning and they say Kylie's leg will be fine. She'll have a little residual stiffness but, with luck, she may well walk again without a limp. And the plastic surgeon is happy with Betty's face. I've told Rod, but he acts as if everything is our fault.'

'I guess he can't accept that the fault's his.'

'No.' Tom sighed. 'I'm afraid he has it in for you, Annie. I can't get it through his thick head that you were legally required to provide the police with a blood sample. Anyway, he's been nil-by-mouth since midnight, and I've given him a pre-med to quieten him down before you anaesthetize him—but you're still in for some invective. I'm sorry.'

'I can handle it.' For heaven's sake, Rod's temper was the least of her problems. 'When do we start?'

'Half an hour.'

'I can do that.' And she set her face and proceeded with her ward round.

Annie discharged Murray, and checked the rest of the patients before Robbie pounced, and pounce he did. She might have known there was no keeping him at bay.

'Am I imagining it, or is there an atmosphere of tension in this hospital this morning?' Robbie demanded as she returned to the nurses' station to fill in Murray's discharge notes. 'And. . . Dr Burrows, are you intending to operate in sunglasses?'

Annie hauled off her glasses and glared at her notes. 'No.'

'So. . . Are you going to tell Uncle Robbie what's wrong?'

'Double no.'

'How about if I pick you up and put you on the filing cabinet and refuse to let you down until you tell me?'

Annie glared.

'You're the nurse, Robbie McKenzie. And I'm the

doctor. The handbook says I'm the one that's supposed to be bossy.'

'Yeah, but I'm still bigger than you.' Robbie smiled down at her, his kindly face sympathetic. 'And, as of this minute, I'm on coffee-break. That means that I'm your friend. Come on, Annie. I can tell you've been having a howl. Ignore the beard and treat me as a mother substitute.'

Annie took a deep breath and looked up at Robbie. He wouldn't leave it, she knew. He had to know some time. Only. . .there was no easy way to say this.

'It's only. . .I'm leaving.'

'Leaving?' Robbie stared. 'You mean. . .leaving Bannockburn?'

'That's right. As soon as T—As soon as Dr McIver can find a replacement.'

'And why would you be doing that?' Robbie's eyes carefully and slowly perused Annie's ravaged face. 'Has our Dr McIver being upsetting you, then?'

'No.'

'No?'

Annie bit her lip. She picked up a patient chart and then put it down again. Chris—the nurse who specialled in romance novels—came into the station and started checking medication sheets. Her ears almost visibly flapped.

And Robbie watched.

The problem with the nurses in this hospital was that they were just too darned good, Annie thought desperately. Tom hand-picked them for their caring natures and their perception, and here it was in force—caring and perception.

Robbie wasn't about to be fobbed off with a half-truth, and neither was Chris. Chris might pretend to be reading medication charts, but Annie knew she was as concerned about Annie's sunglasses as Robbie—and just as determined to know the cause.

So. . . So the truth, the whole truth and nothing but the truth!

'Dr McIver's asked me to marry him,' she said bluntly, and watched two face freeze in shock.

'Bloody hell!' Robbie's jaw dropped a foot or so.

'Oh, Annie!'

'Well. . .' Annie took a deep breath and burrowed her hands deep in the pockets of her white coat. 'You must see how impossible it is for me to work with him after that. So I'm leaving.'

'That's ridiculous.'

'It's what I'm doing.' Annie took a deep breath, grabbed her patient charts and headed for the door— to find her way blocked by Robbie's massive shoulders.

'Are you seriously telling us you'd leave Bannockburn rather than marry our Dr Tom?' he demanded incredulously.

'Rob, don't. . .'

Robbie wasn't listening. A chair was suddenly under Annie. Chris had pushed the swivel chair forward, it had caught Annie under the knees and she'd sat down hard. She was stuck, with two nurses standing over her. Each had one hand on her shoulders—Robbie on one side and Chris on the other—like secret service interrogators.

'Tell us all,' Chris gasped. 'Now! I thought Dr McIver was in love with straw-brained Sarah.'

'He might well be,' Annie said bitterly. 'I wouldn't know. Love's got nothing to do with what he's offering. Can I get up now, please?'

'Not until you've told us everything,' Chris demanded, she and Robbie pushing Annie down again in unison. 'Oh, Annie. . .you and Dr McIver. Wouldn't that be wonderful? Robbie, think about it. . .'

'We could knock the two doctors' apartments into one again.' Robbie grinned his pleasure at the idea. 'They were one big house originally, you know. We had a hell of a time splitting them in two. The bedrooms become one huge living room that looks right out over the river.'

'But. . .'

'And as you have more kids. . .well, we could put an intercom between here and there. Another ward maid to cover the extra work, or a permanent nurse in children's ward. . . Annie, it's perfect.'

'Robbie. . .'

'Oh, and think of the wedding!' Chris looked over at Robbie with stars in her eyes. 'The romance I'm reading now. . . The heroine marries on the beach. . . Bare feet and a simple white dress and her hair hanging free. And the dolphins come in. . . And their two hearts become one. . . Oh, Annie, that's what you should have. A beach wedding. Just like that.'

'I dunno about the dolphins,' Robbie said dubiously. 'I don't think they come to weddings on command. But the rest. . .' His broad face broke into a grin of pure delight. 'Hell, I could even be matron of honour. Just wait until my wife hears about this!'

'Will you two cut it out?' Annie was practically yelling. 'I am *not* marrying Dr McIver!'

One of the domestic staff, scuttling past on early morning collection of menus, cast a startled glance at the trio and scuttled even faster toward the kitchen. Her eyes were as big as saucers.

The news was definitely out.

There'd be no silence in the kitchen now, Annie knew, but there was silence here. Annie sat, wedged between her two interrogators, and glared for all she was worth. Chris and Robbie looked at each other— and took a step back.

'Oh, my dear, of course you are,' Robbie said softly, but there was understanding in his voice as well as pleasure. 'It's such a good idea.'

'For whom?' Annie said bluntly, and Robbie had the nerve to grin again.

'For us, of course. If Dr McIver marries Sarah I'd

imagine he'll live off the premises, and it's much more convenient for us if he lives here.'

'And we don't like Sarah,' Chris said honestly. 'She gives herself airs now. Can you imagine her as the doctor's wife? And if you think any of the other hair-brained twits he's taken out have been any better. . .'

'He picks 'em for their bodies,' Robbie said sagely.

'Well, he didn't pick me because of my body.' Annie rose and backed to the door. 'He picked me because I'll be a good, sensible mother for the family he's envisaging. Our Dr McIver suddenly has a daughter and he realizes it's going to be inconvenient to play sole parent. So. . .so he thinks he'll share the load.'

'Is that how he put it?' Robbie said doubtfully. 'Bloody hell. . .' Clearly he was starting to see where Annie's problem lay.

'So marry him and ask questions later,' Chris said blithely. 'That's what I'd do if someone as dishy as Dr McIver asked me.'

'Yeah, well, no one's likely to because you're a flea-brain,' Robbie said bluntly. 'Annie can't marry him if all he wants is a babysitter.'

'If all he wanted was a babysitter he could have me. Or any one of fifty girls within calling distance.' Chris grinned. 'Annie, I know the paperback romances talk about love and stuff, but honest by. . . Does it really happen in real life? I mean, all the heroes in my books have pecs bigger than footballs—and everything else to match. In real life I've never met any guy like that unless they were out of their brains with steroids. Even Tom McIver has pecs within the normal range. We girls have to take what we can get.'

'But. . .I fell in love with my wife,' Robbie said dubiously, and he reddened under his beard. 'Just like in the books. . .'

'Of course you did.' Annie glared at Chris. 'See? It does happen. There's no earthly reason for me to marry

Tom—and him asking me is an insult. I can't work with him. . .'

'You can work with us, though,' Robbie said, and his voice was suddenly bleak. As if he realized the force of Annie's argument. As if he knew Annie would have to go.

'Oh, of course I can.' Annie's eyes filled with sudden tears and she blinked them away with a fierce effort. She rose and gave Robbie a swift hug, then turned away before her eyes could fill again. 'Or I could until this happened. You're the best workmates. But. . .but I have to go.'

She blinked and made her way down toward Theatre as fast as her legs could carry her.

Tom was already scrubbing.

'So, where's Hannah?' Annie asked as she donned theatre gown and mask. She wasn't about to look at him, but it was hard not to.

'With my housekeeper,' Tom said blandly, and Annie blinked.

'I beg your pardon?'

'You heard,' he told her.

'You didn't have a housekeeper when I went to bed last night,' Annie said cautiously, and Tom grinned behind his mask.

'Nope. I advertised fast.'

'I see.' She didn't see at all. Who was it, then? Sarah? Or the next in line?

'Don't look so suspicious, girl,' Tom complained. 'Cook found her. Edna Harris is fifty-five years old and a happily established widow. Edna intends to grieve placidly for her hubby for the next thirty years. She's not interested in men—but she loves babies. So you haven't been supplanted in my affections.'

'That's amazing,' Annie said dryly. 'I was Sunday's bride. I thought for sure you'd have Monday's edition by now.'

'Annie. . .'

'Rod's ready to go,' Annie said severely, motioning through the open door to where Chris was wheeling in the trolley. 'Maybe we could concentrate on our work?'

'Maybe we could defer this conversation for an hour or so,' Tom agreed. 'But it isn't going to go away, Annie. No matter how hard you try to avoid it.'

The procedure was trickier than expected, for which Annie was profoundly grateful.

First Annie had to anaesthetize Rod—an unpleasant task as he berated her until he lost consciousness. Because Rod Manning was overweight and a smoker, he was tricky to intubate. Then she had to stand not four feet from Tom while he carefully positioned the broken limb, and concentrate on something that wasn't him.

All the time Chris, as theatre nurse, watched Tom and Annie with bright-eyed interest, and Annie knew every look—every nuance—between Tom and herself would be reported happily from one end of the hospital to the other.

Tom had destroyed their working relationship, Annie thought savagely as she finally reversed the anaesthetic. It was finished. She couldn't work with him. It was going to take a superhuman effort to stay here until he could find someone else.

'I'd like you to advertise at once for a replacement,' she told him as Chris wheeled their recovering patient out of Theatre. 'You shouldn't have any trouble getting someone.'

'Your contract is for a year.'

'I'm breaking my contract,' Annie said brusquely. 'If I thought you'd have trouble finding someone then I'd worry, but you won't. So sue me, if you must, but I'm leaving anyway.'

'You don't think your reaction might be just a bit over the top?' Tom said mildly, watching her face. 'I've asked you to marry me, and you've said no. Why the histrionics?'

'I'm not indulging in histrionics.' Annie hauled her theatre gown off and threw it into the laundry basket with more violence than it deserved.

'Annie, I haven't offered you an indecent proposal.' Tom's voice was a study in patience. Experienced doctor coping with hysterical patient. 'I've offered you a sensible and respectable position. It's hardly enough to make you run.'

No. It wasn't. Annie acknowledged the truth of what he said with an inward grimace. But how could she tell him why she was running. . .? She couldn't say, 'It's because I love you, Tom. I can't marry you because I love you. For me, the marriage is no sensible and respectable position. I can't be sensible when I'm near you. And I can't stay here because I love you.' She couldn't.

Instead, she shook her head and headed for the door.

'Annie. . .' Tom caught her wrist and held it. His eyes were suddenly concerned. 'Hell, Annie, what is it?'

'If you don't know. . .'

'Don't know what?'

'That most marriage proposals have the power to change lives,' Annie whispered. 'They change relationships. I can't stay here with you now, Tom. Not now. Not when you've messed everything up. . .'

'By giving you a sensible proposal?'

'How is it sensible?' Annie managed. 'You hardly know me.'

'I do know you, Annie,' Tom told her, and his voice was suddenly dead serious. 'I do. I accept that I haven't seen you as a desirable woman—until yesterday, that is. But I've seen you as a colleague. And what I've seen I like. You're clever. You're kind. You're dedicated to your work and to this hospital. You think about other people and you have a habit of keeping me on the straight and narrow. You're the only woman I know who questions what I do—'

'It sounds like I'd make a great governess,' Annie burst out. 'Not a wife.'

'Maybe I should be the judge of that.'

'I see.' Annie was dangerously close to tears. She fought them back and stood her ground. 'And. . .what sort of husband would you make, Dr McIver? What are you offering?'

'I told you. . . I'd be faithful.'

'I'll adopt Tiny and Hoof if I want faithfulness,' Annie retorted. 'And company. They come with a better track record.'

'Are you offering to take on my dogs?' Tom's ready laughter sprang into his eyes, and Annie backed to the door.

'No way. I'm just saying they'd be as good as you. Better.'

'They eat more. And they snore.'

Was he never serious? Annie winced and reached behind her to open the door.

Chris was still outside in Recovery, standing by Rod's trolley. Her ears were tuned straight to 'receive'.

'Annie, don't go.' Tom stopped her, walking forward and shutting the door on Chris and the outside world again to prevent her leaving. Then he leaned against the door, his long frame dwarfing her and his twinkling eyes looking down with a smile which was nearly her undoing.

'Annie, I'll be a good husband,' he said gently. 'I promise you that. It's true I'm not marrying for romantic reasons. I need. . .I need a mother for my daughter. I need a family. I've suddenly realized that, and I know you haven't made that same decision.

'But I believe a family might suit you, too. It could give us both a stability that's been missing in our lives. I'd be a friend, Annie. Your friend. Someone batting for you. I'd be in your corner—and I'd be in your corner for life. I think that's an offer worth considering.

I know I want you in my corner, Annie, and I'd like to be in yours.'

Annie looked blindly up at him, and it was all she could do not to let her head fall against his chest and hold him tight. . . But he wanted no such thing.

Tom was looking down at her with a look that was earnest, rather than intense, serious, rather than loving—business like.

It was more than Annie could bear.

Somehow, blessedly, anger came to her aid. How dared he put her in this position? She shoved past him with a determination that came of desperation. She had to get out of sight before she thoroughly disgraced herself and slapped his rotten, smiling face—or howled.

'I have three house calls to do this morning,' she said desperately, 'and you have morning clinic. Leave me alone, Tom McIver. Just leave me alone. I suggest we get on with our work—and forget this nonsense ever happened.'

Brave words!

How on earth could Annie forget what had just passed? She hadn't a snowball's chance in a bushfire, she acknowledged as she drove on her morning rounds.

It was just plain impossible. especially as news seemed to travel round Bannockburn even faster than the telephone wires could transmit.

'Is it true?' her first patient asked. Annie had called to check a troublesome ulcer, and Mrs Elder was so excited she was leaning on the front gate, waiting. Normally bed-bound, the old lady was agog.

'They say Melissa Carnem's dumped a baby on our Dr McIver, and now he's decided you'll make a nice wife for him,' the old lady said excitedly as Annie helped her hobble inside. 'Oh, my dear, is it true? My daughter-in-law rang me up not fifteen minutes ago.'

Good grief! It had been a whole two hours since Annie had told anyone! This valley was impossible.

'My dear, I do so hope it is.' Mrs Elder patted Annie's arm and settled back into her chair while Annie unwound the bandages. 'You're such a nice couple— made for each other, I'd say—and it's time that wild young man settled down.'

She smiled at Annie with such affection that Annie blinked.

Oh, dear. . .

The valley might be claustrophobic. There might be solid reasons why she had to get out, but she knew she would desperately miss these people when she had to leave.

She fobbed off Mrs Elder's interest as best she could, and made her way to her next patient. Kirstie Marshal's three-year-old son had earache. Kirstie had six-week-old twins and found it impossible to get to the surgery. She was just as excited as Mrs Elder.

'Sue-Ellen rang and told me,' she said, balancing a twin in one arm and her sad little three-year-old in the other. 'Sue-Ellen's husband delivers the milk to the hospital and they told him this morning. Oh, it's lovely. I can't think why we didn't see it coming. It's such a good idea!'

'You mean it'll settle him down?' Annie asked dourly. She smiled at Kirsty's toddler and lifted him from his mother's grasp. 'Come here, young Matt, and let me see your ear.'

'Well, it can't do any harm.' Kirsty smiled in reminiscence. 'Believe it or not, my Ian used to be a right tearaway. And you should see him now! A nice, steady dad.'

As her 'nice steady dad' chose that moment to stomp through the kitchen attached to muddy gum boots, the second twin started wailing and Matt realized Annie meant business with the auriscope there was little more conversation, but Kirsty and her Ian beamed at her all the way back out to her car.

The valley had wedding bells on the brain.

At least Margaret Ritchie wouldn't be thinking wedding bells, Annie thought, and then grimaced at her thankfulness. That was a small mercy and one she would gladly have done without.

Margaret had terminal bone cancer, and her farmer husband was taking care of her at home. Annie had visited Margaret on the previous Friday and she'd been weak but comfortable, but now Neil Ritchie met her at the back door—and the look on his face was dreadful.

'She's in so much pain. . . Oh, Doc. . . I've given her as much morphine as I dared and now I don't know what to do. We didn't want to trouble you, but we were so glad you were coming. . .'

'What's happened, Neil?'

'I don't know. She got up to go to the bathroom and suddenly she just crumpled. I lifted her back into bed but the pain's something fierce all down her leg.'

'When was this?'

'An hour or so ago.'

He stopped, distress choking his voice. Annie gave his hand a silent squeeze, and made her way swiftly inside.

She stopped in the doorway, recoiling in dismay.

On Friday Margaret had been sitting outside in the sun, but Friday suddenly seemed a long time ago. Now the woman was huddled in her bed like an old, old woman, and her face was contorted in pain. Every few moments a spasm seemed to catch her and her whole body became rigid. Margaret's eyes looked up wildly, pleading for help from anyone—anything—and then she fell back exhausted. She pushed her face into the pillow again, as though trying to hide. . .

'How long has she been like this?' Annie asked, appalled, as she moved swiftly to the bed. 'Oh, Margaret. . . Did you say an hour?'

'Yeah. A bit more,' Neil told her. 'I rang half an hour ago to check you were still coming and they said you were on your way.'

'Neil, I told you to beep me directly if you needed me.' Annie lifted Margaret's wrist and winced at the weakness of her pulse. 'I would have been here in minutes. . .'

'Yeah, but we knew you had others waiting. . .'

That was often the way. The patients who needed help least were the most demanding, and the urgent cases kept their humble place.

'You've given her a boost of morphine?'

'Twice. Ten milligrams an hour ago and another ten just before you arrived.' Neil wiped tears from his face and struggled to make his voice work. 'I wasn't game to give her more.'

'Twenty in all.'

Annie bit her lip in indecision. Tom was in control of Margaret's treatment, and Annie had little experience in the management of cancer pain. Margaret had a syringe driver set up—a mechanism which fed morphine into her body gradually so she didn't suffer the highs and lows of four-hourly injections. Annie lifted the chart and stared. Tom had the driver set at 240 milligrams a day. She did quick conversion into the dosages she was accustomed to—that was forty milligrams every four hours!'

Annie stared helplessly, down frantically trying to think what to do next. Margaret's pain was in her thigh and it didn't take much skill to imagine the probable cause. Annie had seen Margaret's recent X-rays. There was a tumour in the bone. In all probability, the bone would have simply given way and snapped.

The pain was clearly unimaginable.

An ambulance trip to hospital to set it? Yes, but not yet. To move her in such pain was unthinkable. But what else could she do? More morphine? Surely they were at peak dose now, Annie thought bleakly. Any more morphine and Margaret could die under the needle, but as she looked down Annie knew Margaret would count death as a blessing.

And yet. . . Although the cancer in Margaret's bones made her weak and would cause eventual death, she was enjoying the life she had left to her. When Annie had called three days ago, Margaret and Neil had been reading the papers in the sun—gossiping and laughing. Annie had thought Margaret could have up to a year more, please, God. Not like this, she couldn't.

She wouldn't want to live another hour with this pain. In fact, if it wasn't controlled soon she'd go into shock and that alone could kill her.

But the morphine wasn't working.

Why not?

Annie didn't know. She needed help here and she needed it fast. She needed a specialist oncologist or palliative care physician. Or an anaesthetist to block the pain. Or at least a damned good text book. . .

But whatever she needed she needed it now!

'Hold her hand, Neil,' Annie said urgently. 'Tight. Make her aware that help's here. Tell her I'm organizing drug doses. Tell her the pain will stop soon, and tell me where the phone is.'

'And, please, God, let Tom have an answer that I don't,' she said under breath as she headed for the phone. 'Please. . .'

The fact that two hours ago she'd never wanted to see Tom again was forgotten. Now she needed him fast.

At least Tom was available. Rebecca, their receptionist, was fielding calls while Tom conducted Monday clinic. She put Annie straight through and Tom answered on the first ring.

'Hey, Annie.' Tom's voice was strong and warm and welcoming. 'Have you done any reconsidering?'

'Tom, don't. . .' On those two words Annie paused, and by the immediate, listening silence she knew Tom's flippancy was over. As always, when she needed it, she had Tom's instant professional attention.

'What's up?' Tom's voice was suddenly hard, clinical and blessedly steady.

'Margaret Ritchie. . .' Swiftly Annie outlined the problem, and Tom was silent when she finished. Annie didn't question his silence. Her own mind was turning over plan after plan, and she knew Tom's would now be doing the same. He had seven more years medical experience than she. Please let him have an answer.

He did.

'Give her another dose of morphine, Annie,' Tom snapped. 'Now. Thirty milligrams. Do it while I look something up and then come back to the phone.'

'But. . .' Annie gasped. 'Tom, that's almost a hundred milligrams she'll have on board.'

'It won't narcotize while it's working against pain,' Tom explained. 'We can go higher if we have to. Just do it.'

Annie moistened suddenly dry lips. She was being asked to put total professional dependency on Tom here. If Margaret died. . .

She trusted Tom—and there was no choice. Silently she put the phone down and went to do as he said. When she came back to the phone Tom was waiting.

'Two things,' he snapped. 'My oncolgy text says that sometimes with bone cell cancer morphine isn't as effective as other drugs.'

'But—'

Tom was answering her next question before she got it out. 'Naproxen by mouth or rectally if you must—and Panadol as well,' he barked.

'Naproxen. . .'

Naproxen was a non-steroidal anti-inflammatory drug. How would that work if morphine didn't?

'Try it and see, Annie,' Tom ordered. 'I know it's guesswork but, by the sound of it, you have no choice and the text I have is definite. Stay with her and, if you must, give her another dose of morphine. Another thirty milligrams. . .'

'Tom. . .'

'You won't kill her,' Tom reassured her. 'I promise.

Shock from the pain's more likely to kill her. It's only when it's not combating pain that the morphine becomes dangerous. So do it! I'll ring a palliative care physician in Melbourne and check what else to do, then finish here and bring the ambulance out.'

And the line went dead.

Naproxen and Panadol. . .

Annie stared down at the receiver. What a cocktail! On top of that much morphine! A normal, healthy person would die with that combination of drugs.

She had to try. She had no other answers. There wasn't a choice. But if Tom was wrong. . .

With a heavy heart she headed for the car to get what she needed.

It worked.

Just occasionally, in medicine, it was possible to produce a miracle. A really nasty infection pulled up short by antibiotics still had the power to astonish Annie. And this. . . Ten minutes after the first thirty milligrams of morphine was injected, the spasms of pain started losing power. The pain was still bad so Annie took Tom at his word and injected more. Within an hour the naproxen and Panadol started to do their work.

Margaret's body sagged in exhausted relief and, still clutching her hand, Neil Ritchie burst into tears.

'Oh, girl. . . Oh, Doc, you've done it. Dear God, I thought I was losing her.' He slumped back into a chair and put his head in his hands.

'I think Margaret intends sticking round for a while yet.' Annie smiled, almost dizzy with relief herself, and took Margaret's thin hand from Neil. 'You agree, Margaret?'

Margaret stared speechlessly up at her, exhausted beyond belief, but her frail fingers gripped and held.

'How goes it?'

Annie spun round to find Tom in the doorway. Her relief was so great that if Margaret hadn't been holding her hand she could have crossed the room and kissed him! Or agreed to marry him on the spot.

'Here's the man we have to thank,' she whispered, her voice almost as shaken as Neil's. 'Dr McIver told me what to do. Tom, it worked! How on earth. . .? I just don't understand. . .'

'It's just getting the right cocktail mix—and I've spent years of my life studying cocktails.' Tom grinned and carefully placed what he was carrying—one baby capsule—on the floor beside the door. He smiled at them all, and crossed the room to grasp Neil's shaking shoulders in a strong grip of comfort.

'Hey, Neil, you look sicker than your wife. Take it easy.' Then his eyes met Annie's, warm and strongly reassuring. 'Morphine works against most pain but occasionally it doesn't. According to my text—and the physician I rang backs it up—bone pain is one thing it can sometimes not be effective for. Luckily, when it doesn't work naproxen usually does. I gather it's been effective.'

'You can't imagine,' Margaret whispered weakly.

'I think I can.' Tom looked from Annie's face to Neil's and then back to Margaret. 'Bone pain is just bloody! Annie, have you done an examination yet?'

'No.' Annie shook her head. 'I didn't want to stir any more pain. I'd guess the leg's broken but we'll need to do an X-ray.'

'I'm not going to hospital,' Margaret said fiercely, and Tom smiled.

'Not even for a quick visit? All we'll do is X-ray your leg, and if it's fractured—as we suspect—then we'll pin it. That's the long-term solution for this fierce pain.'

'The long-term. . .?'

'You're not going to die on us yet, Margaret,' Tom said gently. 'I think the time's come when we need to look at a wheelchair, but the modern wheelchair is a wonderful thing. You'll be able to round the cows up

with Neil, no sweat!' His smile faded. 'Margaret, Annie
said you'd been in pain for over an hour before she
came. Why didn't you and Neil call us?'

'We. . .we didn't want. . .'

'To bother anyone.' Tom finished the sentence for
her and crossed to sit on her bed. He took the hand
that Annie wasn't holding, linking the three of them
together.

'Margaret, you and Neil have decided to cope with
your illness at home. That's great. You should have
months—maybe years—of peaceful life before you.
And Annie and I agree that whatever treatment you
need will be given at home. But it's conditional,
Margaret. Our help is conditional.'

'On. . .on what?'

'On you calling us when you need us. The minute
you need us. On you treating us as if we're no further
than the telephone and we're sitting idle and waiting
for your call. If you don't do that, Margaret, then it
makes it impossible for you, impossible for Neil and
impossible for us.'

'But. . .'

'Look at Annie's face, Margaret,' Tom said sternly.
'And look at your husband's. They both look like
they've been through the wringer. When you suffer we
suffer, and if you don't let us help then it punishes
us. It doesn't inconvenience us if you call. It hurts if
you don't.'

He squeezed her hand and rose. 'Dave's outside with
the ambulance, and we'll move you now and get this
leg fixed,' he told her. 'By the look of you, you're close
to sleep, and there's nothing to stop you from sleeping
through the next couple of hours while we X-ray and
pin the leg, if we need to. Sleep, and we'll do our work
while you're sleeping.' He smiled. 'But before you drift
off. . .I brought someone to meet you.'

Margaret was so exhausted she was almost past

speaking, but her eyes moved instinctively from Tom's face to the floor by the door.

'You brought. . .'

'I brought my daughter.'

Tom walked to the door and scooped up his little girl from her capsule. Hannah was fast asleep, her tiny body limp and peaceful in Tom's big hands. Tom lifted the baby high in a gesture of love and pride that made Annie gasp.

It seemed at long last that Tom McIver was falling in love—with his tiny daughter.

Annie watched, tears pricking behind her eyes, as he carried the baby over to the bed and laid her on the coverlet. He stood back as Margaret reached to touch the tiny, sleeping face.

'Oh, Tom, she's so like you,' Margaret whispered, and her face which, minutes before, had been contorted in pain relaxed in pleasure. 'And she's perfect. . .'

'Isn't she?' Tom scooped up his daughter again, cradling her against his chest. He looked down into the baby's sleeping face and his eyes reflected his pride. 'Sleep now, Margaret—but I sort of hoped you might like to see her.'

He'd thought this through, Annie thought in amazement, intensely moved. Tom must have checked his texts, talked to the physician and decided Margaret's pain could be alleviated—and then he'd thought to what lay ahead. Now, instead of sleeping with the thought that the pain might return—that something else might break—Margaret was being given something new to think about. There could be no better ending to a morning of terror than the gift of new life.

'If you like, from now on we'll bring her whenever we come to see you,' Tom told Margaret. 'Either Annie or I. . .'

'It's true, then?' Margaret was fading fast toward sleep, whispering with her eyes almost closed. It was all Annie could do to hear her. 'Ellen Elder rang—just as things were getting really bad—and said you and Annie were getting married.' Her eyes closed completely. 'I can't think. . .I can't think of anything I'd look forward to more. The marriage of two people who deserve each other. . .'

And she drifted off to sleep.

CHAPTER EIGHT

'THE WHOLE VALLEY thinks it's a good idea,' Tom said plaintively. 'You're the odd man out.'

'They do not!' said Annie. 'Have you asked Sarah?'

'That's hitting below the belt.'

'Have you?'

'I don't know why Sarah should object. Sarah doesn't want to marry me.'

'Neither do I. Now could you concentrate on what you're doing or we'll have Mrs Reilly suing us for removing the wrong bit.'

Tom chuckled, unmoved.

'She wouldn't miss anything. Mabel Reilly hasn't seen anything below the waist since she hit sixteen stone many years ago. I doubt she'd notice if we whipped off a leg and attached a wooden one instead. She'd only complain that the floors sound noisy.'

Chris giggled from the other side of the table. The young nurse was thoroughly enjoying what was happening between Annie and Tom. The whole of Bannockburn was enjoying it! Chris handed Tom a suture and beamed.

'I think it's about time you two sorted things out,' she pronounced with authority. 'We all do. It's been two weeks, Dr Burrows, and you haven't given the man an answer.'

'I have given the man an answer,' Annie said darkly. 'It's just not the one he wants.'

'It's not the one anyone wants.' Chris gave Tom a conspiratorial grin. 'Dr Burrows, Dr McIver's right when he says everyone wants you to marry him.'

'Would I be marrying Dr McIver—or the valley?'

'The valley,' Chris said promptly. 'You couldn't leave then.'

'And you'd all have a nice, steady doctor for years.' Annie concentrated on her dials with a ferociousness that a simple gallstone removal in a healthy fifty-year-old didn't warrant. 'I just wish everyone would get off my back. Especially you, Dr McIver.' She managed a speedy glare between scrutinizing dials. 'And I know you haven't done the first thing about advertising my position—but I'm leaving at the end of the month, whether you've bothered to find a replacement or not!'

Tom just gave an infuriating grin—but Chris gasped.

'You can't mean that?' Chris sounded outraged.

Annie lifted a syringe and had to collect herself before she plunged it home with more force than it deserved.

'I do,' she pronounced savagely. 'The whole valley's blackmailing me into this marriage—and I can't see a single thing in it for me. Nothing!'

'You can't mean it.'

Chris's question was repeated when Helen found Annie that night, sitting in Children's Ward beside a little boy suffering from a spider bite. The spider was a white tail, which meant there was little danger to the child's life but that particular spider's bite had a nasty habit of making the skin around the bite die if it wasn't treated with care.

The child's parents were dairy farmers and hadn't been able to come in tonight so Annie, with time on her hands, had sat with him until he'd slept.

'I can't mean what?' Annie was a million miles away. Now she stirred, and turned to find that the night sister had obviously been watching her for a while.

'Chris says you don't believe there's anything in this marriage for you.'

'That's right.'

'No.' Helen hauled up a chair and sat down beside

her, with the air of a woman ready to sit it out. 'It's wrong. Annie, maybe it's time you and I talked.'

'Talk all you like,' Annie said bitterly. 'The whole valley's talking. They've been talking of nothing else for two weeks.'

'They have, you know,' Helen said gently. 'They've been talking of the change that's come over Dr McIver since his baby arrived. They've been watching as he carts the little one around like a man who's been granted something he never thought he'd have. He has his housekeeper, but his little girl's spending more time with her daddy than with Edna. Dr McIver's been knocked sideways by his little daughter, and you must see it.'

'I suppose. . .' Annie shrugged, grudgingly conceding the point. 'I suppose he has.' She thought back to the Tom she was seeing around the hospital. 'I guess he seems more peaceful.'

'He does that.' Helen smiled. 'The man's been like a coiled spring since I've known him. Filling every moment with activity. This evening when I came on duty I found them both out in the hospital garden—Tom and his daughter—lying under the gum trees waiting for the evening star to appear. Tom was explaining the heavens to his daughter. They didn't see me and I wouldn't have intruded for the world—but, oh, my dear, it made me feel lumpy inside to see it.'

'Yeah, well. . .'

'It makes you feel like that, too, doesn't it?' Helen asked softly, and when Annie didn't answer she put a hand on hers.

'You love him, Annie.'

'I. . .'

'Don't lie to me,' Helen told her. 'I've watched you. I know you love Tom McIver. That's why I told him he should marry you.'

'You. . .'

'The night of the accident,' Helen told her. 'He was

wandering round like a stunned mullet, trying to figure
out just what he should do. He was still talking about
marrying Sarah. I told him that if he wanted someone
who'd turn him into part of a family he shouldn't look
past you.'

'Yeah. He didn't even think of it himself,' Annie
said bitterly, and Helen gave a sad little smile.

'He couldn't. Something happened in the past that
makes him wary of commitment. That's why he's gone
from one unsuitable girl to the next. That's why. . .
that's why he has to marry with his head—and find
that love will come later.'

'Helen. . .'

'He thought the idea ridiculous when I told him,'
Helen went on, ignoring Annie's interruption. 'But
then. . .halfway through your picnic he said he suddenly
saw what I'd been seeing all along. That you're true
and kind and loving—and you'd make him a much
better wife than any of these nincompoops he's been
escorting. So. . .'

'So he made a decision with his head.'

'That's right.' Helen's voice firmed. 'He has. And
you love him. So it's up to you to marry him and teach
him to love you back. You can do it, Annie. If I didn't
think you could I would have shut up in the first place.
But I think this marriage has a far better chance of
working than many where the only thing the bride and
groom have going for them is romantic love. You love
the real Tom McIver, Annie. And he's worth the risk!'

'Helen, I can't. . .'

'You can, you know,' Helen said gently. 'And I wish
you would.' She stood. 'But, meanwhile, Mr Whykes
is unsettled and I need an order for diazepam—if it's
OK with you, Doctor?' And her request was so meek
that Annie burst out laughing.

'I don't believe you need doctors at all in this
hospital, Sister. Just signatures. You organize us all.'

'I try,' Helen said meekly. 'You and Dr McIver first. Chris next. She's on my list.'

'Poor Chris.' Annie rose and looked down searchingly at the sleeping child. 'Bobby won't wake until morning. I'll come and see Mr Whykes. Does he need sedation? He's been much more settled.'

'I know. But Robbie said one of his sons brought in the farm books this afternoon for him to go over. He thoroughly enjoyed telling them all how badly managed the finances had been since he'd been in hospital. He spent too much time with pen and paper and is now paying the consequences.'

Helen put a hand on Annie's shoulder and pressed her back down onto her chair. 'There's no need for you to come. Verbal order and sign later. You sit there—and think about what I've just said. Think, Annie. Because if you don't take this risk—if you don't marry the man you love—you may just regret it for the rest of you life.'

'Marry him, dear.'

Margaret Ritchie was lying on a settee on the verandah when Annie called the next day. And, as per orders, Annie had brought Hannah. The baby gurgled and chirped on Margaret's coverlet and then subsided into delighted silence as Annie produced a bottle.

'Do you take her with you often?' Margaret asked, and Annie shook her head.

'Only here.' She smiled. 'Tom takes her everywhere. His dogs are too jealous for words.'

'Will they be jealous of you, do you think? When you marry him?'

'Margaret. . .'

'Don't tell me.' Margaret reached out and touched Annie's hand. She was pain-free now and the lines around her face had softened and eased. This lady would face death with dignity and courage when her time came—but her time was a long way off yet. 'Don't tell me you're not brave enough.'

'Margaret, he doesn't love me!'

'But do you love him?'

Silence. Neil had left them alone. There were only the two women in the soft afternoon sun—and one feeding baby.

The answer lay between them as clearly as if it had been spoken.

'I see,' Margaret said gently. She looked down at the sleepy Hannah. 'And this little one. . . Do you think you could love her, too?'

Annie looked down at the tiny cluster of brown curls on Hannah's head, and she felt her heart twist. It was strange. She'd never thought she'd have children. Tom's vision of her future—as an elderly spinster doctor—was pretty much how Annie had seen herself. But this little one. . . Somehow Hannah had twisted her way round her heart, and Annie knew she had feelings for her as she had for no other.

Maybe it was because she was so much a part of Tom. . .

'And what about his dogs?'

Margaret's voice was insistent, and for the first time Annie found herself smiling.

'Tiny and Hoof. . . What woman would be crazy enough to take them on?'

'I think you would,' Margaret said softly. 'I think you should.'

'Margaret, he doesn't love me.'

'He doesn't know what he wants,' Margaret said. 'It might take a bit of age and experience to see that but, in a way, I think Tom McIver is as confused as you are. And with this marriage. . .' She shook her head.

'Annie, life isn't a dress rehearsal. Look at me. I'm not quite sixty, and it's almost over. But I've had my Neil, my children, my farm and my life—and there's not one thing I've done that I've regretted. I've made mistakes but I've taken every opportunity that's come my way—grasped it with open hands—and I'm so glad

I did. Sure, Tom McIver might cause you heartaches, but what's the alternative?'

'Margaret. . .'

'Marry him, dear!'

Marry him. . .

Annie spent the rest of the day working on automatic pilot. She did her afternoon clinic and was fortunate that there was little except coughs and colds and the odd sprain or stitch. After dinner she took herself for a long walk on the beach. She returned after dark and sat alone in her flat, listening to Tom talk to his baby and his dogs.

As Hannah settled, Annie took her courage in both hands—and walked the few steps to his door.

Tom answered on the second knock, and his dogs tumbled out behind him to greet her. Two dogs and one doctor. Three males, almost as big as each other. All with the same silly grins.

'Annie. . .'

'Can I talk to you?'

Tom's grin faded. He shoved his dogs back inside and closed the door.

'What is it, Annie? What's wrong?'

Annie took a deep breath. And then another one.

'I've decided,' she said at last, in a voice that trembled. She stared down at the floor. 'If you still want me to. . . Tom, if you think it's a good idea, I'll marry you.'

Silence.

And then, very slowly, Tom pulled her into his arms.

'That's great, Annie,' he said, and she could feel his breath against her hair. 'That's fantastic. You won't regret it. Between us, I think we've made a really sensible decision.'

CHAPTER NINE

SENSIBLE!

That was the last word Annie would have used to describe her decision, and it was the last word she *could* use to describe the way the valley reacted to the news. The valley erupted into something that wavered between hysteria and delirium, she decided, as her request for no fuss was met with blank rejection.

'No way,' Chris declared.

'If I can't be matron of honour, I quit,' Robbie announced. Margaret Ritchie even sent off to Melbourne for a new dress.

'Because I won't miss your wedding for the world, my dear,' she told Annie. 'No one will. If we're not invited I think you'll have every head in the valley poking in the church windows and singing along with the hymns.'

'Oh, you're invited,' Annie said, and she couldn't quite keep a note of panic from creeping into her voice. 'I want you to come especially, Margaret, but you'd be coming, anyway. Tom's invited everyone from here to Timbuktu. If you've ever been on a mailing list or in a telephone book then you're invited.'

'Annie, stop panicking.'

Tom found her in her office later that afternoon. She'd fled there to escape the wedding buzz around the hospital.

Legally there was a four-week waiting period for marriage, but Tom would wait no longer than he had to. So. . . They'd been engaged for two weeks, there were two weeks to go before the wedding and Annie didn't see how the fuss could get any greater.

In the hospital kitchen there were pink and white rosettes being made instead of cakes for the patients' supper.

'It won't hurt the patients to have bought biscuits until the wedding,' Cook informed her. 'Everyone understands.'

They surely did. There were even a couple of patients tying pink and white ribbons.

Annie retreated to Intensive Care, only to find that Chris was sitting by Mrs Christianson's bed, checking monitors and stitching her bridesmaid's dress at the same time.

So she'd fled.

'The whole hospital's mad,' Annie muttered, bending over her work. 'Tom, this is crazy.'

'Annie!' Tom leaned over her desk and put his palms flat on her prescription pad, effectively stopping her writing. 'If we're going to get married we might as well have the works. I only intend to do this once in my life. Besides, it'll mean you have to take your jeans off for the day.' And he kissed her on the top of her head.

Yeah, great! He was still treating her as a kid sister. Would he always?

Annie looked up doubtfully at the man before her and, as always, she felt a lurch of something she could never understand. Tom was white-coated, professional and self-assured. The full medical bit. He looked like a medical colleague, but there was no way Annie could see him as such.

She was so full of doubts, but it seemed there were no doubts for Tom. Tom McIver was in charge of his world again, and ever since Annie had agreed to marry him he hadn't stopped grinning.

'Tom, it seems stupid. To have the full romantic bit when we're not—'

'We're not what? Romantic?' Tom kicked the door closed, seized her face and gave her a light kiss on the lips. 'We can be as romantic as you like. So. . .how romantic would you like to be?'

With an effort, Annie pulled herself free.

'Don't be silly, Tom.'

'I'm not being silly.' He didn't mind her pulling away, though. He dropped into a chair on the other side of her desk and watched her with complacency. Tom had her where he wanted her, and he wasn't pushing his luck. 'Speaking of romance, though. . . How about a honeymoon? If I get a locum, shall we take ourselves to Tahiti?'

'What, with Hannah and Hoof and Tiny?' Annie hauled another patient's file towards her and flipped it open. 'You go on a honeymoon, Tom McIver. I'm too busy.'

'You sound crabby.'

'I feel crabby.'

'Why?' Tom asked blandly—and Annie had to find an answer.

'Because I'm being bulldozed into white lace and confetti.'

'You really, truly, don't want it? A proper wedding?' Tom folded his arms and fixed her with a look.

And Annie couldn't say no. She couldn't. She stared at the paper in front of her and thought of saying what she really thought—that a full bridal and a honeymoon with Tom were things she'd dreamed of for years and now she'd gone this far she couldn't pull back, but that the dream wasn't complete.

But, of course, the words couldn't come. If they had Tom would walk away right now, she thought sadly. She'd scare him silly. Tom wanted an independent partner. A sensible match. Not some clinging vine. . .

'I. . .I had a letter from Rod Manning's solicitor,' she managed finally, retreating back to medicine as fast as she could.

'Rod. . .' Tom frowned, blessedly distracted. 'What does he want?'

'He wants a copy of his treatment notes.' Annie rose to look out the window. Tom at her desk was, well, he was too close for comfort.

'Why?'

'I think Rod's trying to figure a way he can sue me,' Annie said heavily. 'He hates me.'

'Surely not.' Tom's frown deepened. 'The man must be reaching paranoid stage. It's more than a month since the accident. He should be coming to terms with it by now.'

'I don't think so.'

'And he's upsetting you? Is that what's wrong?' Tom rose, walked around to where she stood and placed his hands on her shoulders. Against her better judgement, Annie felt herself lean back against him. His body felt so good. It felt so right. 'Annie, I'm sure there's no need to worry. I agree, the solicitor's letter demanding the notes is ominous, but he might have some other reason for wanting them. Maybe insurance. . .'

With an effort, Annie managed to keep her voice working. The way he was holding her. . .she could almost imagine herself cherished. 'I don't. . .I don't think so.' She sighed, giving in to the feel of Tom's hands.

'Kylie and Betty are OK—but gossip says Betty's asking for a divorce. It seems the accident was the last straw. Rod's been drinking heavily and knocking her around. On the night of the ball Betty knew he shouldn't be driving—but he was so abusive that she went with him against her better judgement. So now. . . Rod hasn't just lost his licence. He's lost his family.'

'I see.' Tom was kneading her shoulders gently and Annie's body had started to do strange things. She was growing warm from the thighs up. 'His world has been blown apart—and it's easier to blame you than himself.' Tom's voice was as gentle as his hands, infinitely comforting. 'Annie, none of that is your fault. Rod did it to himself.'

'I guess I know that. I rang medical defence and asked them to check my notes, and they're happy I acted properly. I had no choice but to give the police the blood sample so I've sent the notes on to Rod's lawyer. With luck, his lawyer will tell Rod the same story—that I didn't have a choice in giving the police the blood sample—and that'll be an end to it.'

'I don't like it, though.' Tom pulled her tightly against him, her back curved into his chest. He was becoming more possessive—more patriarchal—by the minute. 'Rod has a violent temper. You keep out of his way.'

'Yes, sir. . .'

It was a mocking rejoinder but it made Tom hold her tighter.

'You're my future wife. As of Saturday week. No one threatens my family.'

'No.' The word was a faint, bleak little reply that no one could understand except Annie.

She was being stupid, she told herself. Tom was offering what most girls would kill for. He was offering her his name and his protection.

And he'd love her—in a way. She knew that. It was already happening. He'd love her as he loved Hoof and Tiny—he'd love her because she was part of the family he was creating. But what that love lacked had everything to do with the dull ache around her heart.

He'd have loved Sarah if he'd thought she was suitable. Or Melissa. Or someone else. . .

Annie just wanted him to love her for herself, sensible or not. For her. For Annie.

It was stupid wish. Fairy tales happened between the covers of books. They didn't happen to Annie Burrows.

Tom kissed her on her nape—a kiss of light affection. 'OK, Annie, as long as you stop worrying I'm off. I'm taking Hannah and the dogs to the beach so I'll see you later.'

He kissed her again lightly on the cheek—a kiss of affection and farewell—and he left her.

Annie was left staring at a closed door. And the panic welled up all over again.

Tom was taking Hannah and the dogs to the beach. He was taking *his family*. But he wasn't taking Annie.

He hadn't thought of asking if she wanted to go, and there was no reason why he should. Tom had done his courting. He had what he wanted.

But. . . The hospital was quiet. If they took the mobile phone there was no reason why Annie shouldn't go to the beach with them. If they'd wanted her.

It was her own fault, she thought sadly. She'd consented to be his wife. There was no need to court her any more. No need at all when one essential element to a marriage was missing. Tom's love.

Annie slumped down in her chair again, despair rising within her. Dear God, what was she letting herself in for?

The wedding was perfect.

It didn't have a choice. Every person in the valley contributed. Even Tiny and Hoof were groomed to canine perfection. They stood to attention on either side of the entrance to the chapel, and they hardly needed the children Tom had assigned to hold them.

Annie had been right in her guess at numbers. Every person in the telephone book was there—plus a few more!

Much to Chris's disgust, they had a traditional church wedding.

'Beach weddings are fine when you only have young, healthy guests,' Tom said definitively when Chris told him her plans for sea and dolphins, 'but I want the whole valley to come. Grandmas and grandpas and people with prams and—'

'You really are making a public statement that you're starting something big,' Chris said curiously, and watched Annie's face. Annie had been growing more and more quiet as the day approached.

And on the day itself she was almost dumbstruck.

Chris and Helen dressed her in a gown made by Chris's mum—and Annie gazed in the mirror and hardly knew herself.

A vision flashed through of the girl she'd seen once before. The student who'd worn a ball gown for the first time and had been derided by her family for being ridiculous.

As soon as they'd opened their mouths, that was how she'd felt. Ridiculous. Well, neither her mother nor her sister were here today. Her sister was overseas on a modelling assignment and her mother was taken up with some new man.

But their words stayed with her.

'I don't. . . Helen, I can't. . .'

'Of course you can.' Helen twisted her around so that Annie was staring straight at the mirror. 'You must. If you think we can waste this. . .'

Annie stared. This wasn't Annie.

The gown was deceptively simple—soft silken organza with a sweetheart neckline, tiny sleeves and a bodice that curved around her breasts as if it was moulded to her. As, indeed, it was. The front of the dress was simplicity itself, but at the back silk lacing ran from where the neck scooped low at the neckline to where soft folds billowed out from her tiny waistline to fall in soft clouds to the floor.

There were no frills. The dress was designed to show Annie as she really was—not some designer version of what a bride should be. Chris and Helen tumbled her shining curls softly around her shoulders and a wreath of tiny white rosebuds drifted through her hair. In her hands Annie held a posy of the same white rosebuds. Her eyes were huge in her face, and it was a face Annie had never seen before.

'Oh, I wish Hannah was old enough to be a flower

girl,' Chris breathed. 'Not that you need one. Annie, you're quite beautiful.'

'I'm not beautiful.'

'If you don't think you're beautiful then you must be blind,' Chris retorted. 'And don't tell me you are blind. You know you don't really need those awful glasses, and why you wear them. . .I think I'll toss them into the river now we've finally got them off you.' She linked her arm in Annie's. 'Enough. Helen and I have decided there'll be discussion on this subject after you're safely hitched, but for now. . . For now, Dr Burrows, Matron Robbie is waiting to give you away. And if anyone catches your bouquet except me, I'll just *die*.'

And then events overtook them.

There was so little of her wedding day Annie remembered.

Snatches.

A chapel bursting with people. The dogs, smirking as if they'd planned the whole thing. Tom's housekeeper, coming forward with Hannah——beaming her pleasure and placing the baby in Annie's arms for a brief photogenic moment before she went into church. Flashbulbs popped everywhere, and afterwards there were pictures of Annie, holding her new little stepdaughter, pinned on walls all over the valley.

Hannah gurgling up with pleasure as if this new arrangement was entirely to her satisfaction.

Margaret Ritchie in a wheelchair just inside the church, reaching forward to grip Annie's hand before Rob led Annie proudly down the aisle.

'My dear, this is the best thing. . .for you both. . . Savour every moment.'

She couldn't. She couldn't even think.

The wedding march blared forth.

And then Annie looked ahead, to find Tom smiling at her like the proverbial Cheshire cat. He looked impossibly handsome in his black dinner suit, his eyes

on hers—as if he sensed her panic—impossibly gentle
and kind.

How could she not want to marry this man? He'd
asked it of her, and she could give him this one thing.
Give him herself.

Only. . .

Tom wanted just a part of her. He didn't demand the
part she was longing to give.

She took a deep breath, and then Rob was leading
her forward. The smile on Robbie's face matched
Tom's. The valley had made this match, Rob's grin
said, and the valley folk were seeing it through.

Annie let him take her forward until another hand
came out to claim her—and she turned to become
Tom's wife.

Day misted into night. There was a feast to end all
feasts, and dancing out under the stars.

As the night grew old Tom pulled his bride into his
arms and held her close.

'OK, my lovely, lovely Annie. Time to leave this
lot to enjoy themselves. Time for bed.'

'Bed?' Annie flashed a look up at him that was half-
scared—the rest of her was just plain terrified. 'Tom. . .'

'It's customary, you know,' he teased. 'The best of
couples do it on their wedding night. I know we decided
against a honeymoon, but for tonight, well, there's two
of my doctor mates who are currently dancing their legs
off with Chris and Sarah, but they've promised to look
after medical emergencies. Edna's caring for Hannah.
And I've even boarded out Hoof and Tiny. What greater
sacrifice can a man make?'

What, indeed?

Annie looked helplessly up at him. She was way out
of her depth—scared stiff of crossing boundaries she
could hardly see. There were no rules for the game she
was playing.

How to love a man and yet not love him.

How to need him so much that her heart was dissolving at the thought of him needing her—and yet not let him see her need.

And how to cope with the fact that she was a sensible wife. A wife of necessity.

'Don't worry, my Annie,' Tom whispered, pulling her into his arms and holding her close. He misunderstood the reason for her panic entirely. 'I won't hurt you. I'll never hurt you.'

But will you ever love me like I want to be loved? Annie thought longingly, as Tom wove his way through the dancers, holding tight to his bride at his side and laughing a goodnight to their guests.

Will you, Tom?

He made a good start.

Annie woke to bliss. There were no words to describe how she felt. She lay curled in the protective line of Tom's body, his arms holding her close, and she thought if she could die now there could be nothing more she could ask for.

She might be a wife of necessity—but last night she had felt truly loved. Tom had taken her to him as something of infinite worth. She had felt beautiful and wondrous and cherished, and her body had melted into Tom's as if they'd been made for each other.

Her husband. . .

She looked up into his face and she felt her heart stir with overwhelming love. Maybe this could work. Please. . .

He opened his eyes and looking down at her, and his eyes were as gentle and loving as she could possibly hope. And possessive. She was his wife, his look said. His. 'Awake, my Annie?'

'Mmm.'

He kissed her on the forehead—and then bent to kiss her full on the mouth. Annie felt her lips tremble under his, and as his kiss deepened heat surged through her

body as she responded to all the love inside her. Like
a bud unfurls to the sun, she responded to this man.
Her love.

She put her arms around him and held him close—
his naked body against hers—and just for this once she
let all her pent-up longing explode into aching need.
Her body arched into his and she felt his body react
with disbelief—and then with absolute delight.

'My God, I've married a wanton. . .'

'Wanton. . . Wanting you. . .'

'I didn't hurt you last night, did I?'

She'd surprised him, she knew. He'd expected her
to be as reluctant as the look of panic she'd worn on
her face when he'd led her to bed had suggested.
Only. . .the panic wasn't that he'd love her. The panic
was that he wouldn't.

Would I be coming back for more if you'd hurt me?'

'Are you coming back for more?' He kissed
her again.

In answer, Annie's fingers drifted downward. . .
down. . .until they found what they were seeking. And
there was no mistaking what she felt.

He did want her, her fingers told her. Love her or
not, for this moment she was his woman—his wife—
and he wanted her in the age-old way a man had loved
a woman from the beginning of time. If she had to be
content with that then so be it.

She'd made her bed and now she'd lie in it. She'd
take what she could get, and fight for more.

'Oh, yes,' she breathed, and she let her fingers do
her pleading for her. 'If you'll have me, Tom McIver,
then I'm yours.'

It couldn't last.

Their honeymoon came to an end mid-morning when
the rest of the world broke in. Tom's medical mates
had to return to the city, and without them Tom or
Annie was needed. There was a hospital to run.

The farmer who'd cared for Tiny and Hoof drove by and released them in the hospital grounds. He obviously hadn't given them breakfast and they were displeased. They signalled their return by attempting to scratch Tom's door down.

Edna rang to say she'd run out of formula and would they like her to bring Hannah home?

Tom had a fast shower, while Annie lay in his bed and tried to come to terms with her new status. Her new life. She watched through the bathroom door as Tom showered, marvelling at his wonderful body—the body that held the promise of pleasure to come.

'You look like the cat that got the cream.' Tom smiled down at his wife as he hauled his shirt on. Annie lay still under the sheets, sated and drowsy. Holding onto this moment for as long as she could. 'But the cat had best stir. The world calls.'

'The world's coming right in if you don't open that door,' Annie retorted, smiling back at her love. 'Tiny and Hoof between them are a match for any barricade.'

Then she hesitated, thinking of nights to come. If she stayed here. . . She was sleeping in Tom's bed. There was no separate bedroom in his apartment for Hannah, or for the two dogs.

'Tom, do you want to do something about the apartments?'

'What?' Tom looked around his bedroom as if he were seeing it for the first time. 'What's wrong with it? Do we need a bigger bed, do you think? This is about as big as they come.'

'I mean. . .' Annie hesitated, searching for courage. 'Tom, Robbie suggested, we knock down the wall between the apartments. Make them into one big house.'

Silence.

Tom carefully buttoned his shirt, hauled on his pants and sat on the bed to put his shoes on. He didn't look at her.

'Let's wait, Annie,' he said at last.

'Wait?'

'Well, I agree we should put a door between us. But one house. . .'

'You don't like the idea?'

'Well, it's just that we're two independent people.' He shrugged, then leaned back and lifted her curls, tumbling over her pillows. 'I don't say that I'll get tired of you, Annie, but. . .well, there may be times when we do want to be apart.' He kissed her on the nose.

'I see.'

'You agree?' He was looking at her as if she couldn't help but agree. After all, it wasn't as if she was in love with the man—was she?

'Of course.'

Flat. Sensible. The return to earth of Annie Burrows.

'Fine, then.' Tom took himself off to the mirror to comb his hair.

The world calls. . .

Annie swung her legs over the side of the bed, hauling the sheet with her, and Tom watched her in the mirror and laughed.

'Modesty? Where was that an hour ago?'

When I was pretending that you really wanted me as your wife. Annie thought her reply, but she couldn't say it.

'There's work to be done, Tom McIver. If you spend any more time preening in front of the mirror I'll have to take over your patients as well as mine.'

'Preening?' He winced. 'Ouch.' He shook his head. 'Annie, once a day, whether I need it or not, I stand in front of the mirror and do my hair. Also I shave. Your definition of preening. . .'

'Preening,' she said flatly, half-teasing. 'Sheer vanity!'

'Well, maybe it's time you learned about vanity.' With a grin of pure mischief, Tom stalked out into the corridor and into the apartment next door. She heard him moving round in her bedroom—and then he

marched right back. In his arms he carried the entire
contents of her wardrobe which he proceeded to dump
on the bedroom floor.

'Watch,' he told her firmly.

Then, while Annie stared, dumbfounded, he marched
out to his kitchenette and came back with two large
bottles. Before Annie could realize what he intended
he'd upended them over the lot.

Annie's jaw dropped about a foot.

'You. . .' Annie stared speechlessly. 'Tom. . .' She
made a dive for the pile but Tom was before her. He
swept her off her feet, her sheet slipped sideways and
he dumped her naked body back on the bed.

'No, you don't,' he told her kindly, his eyes dancing
with wickedness. 'If you knew how long I've been
aching to do that. . . The big bottle was soy sauce and
the bigger one's bleach from Theatre. Double strength.
Let the bleach do its job. Ten minutes and even *you*
won't wear them.'

'You have no right!'

'I'm your husband.' He grinned. 'In days gone by I
could have bumped you on the head with a club and
dragged you back to my cave by the hair. Or installed
you as wife number eight and made you pregnant
fifteen times.

"I've thought it all out. I'm doing none of those things
because I'm a civilized male—and because, of course,
we're equal. But this once, Annie. . .this one time. . .I
figured I don't want a wife in old T-shirts two sizes
too big for her, and the only way to avoid that is to be
ruthless.'

'Ruthless. . .' Annie hauled her sheet back around
her and glared up in fury. 'Tom, if you don't like my
clothes then you didn't have to marry me.'.

'But you fit my criteria in every other way.' He
smiled, and the dangerous twinkle that had been Annie's
undoing gave her a message of pure sensuality. A look
to make her toes curl! 'And very exacting criteria they

are, too. Annie, you are a truly beautiful woman and
yesterday you took my breath away. So. . . Helen and
Chris and I. . .'

'Helen and Chris. . .'

'I like being wicked in a team.' Tom chuckled. 'Then
I can say it was all their idea.'

'Was it?'

'No. I decided—'

'You decided what?' Annie could hardly speak. Her
nice, controlled world was tilting on its axis at such a
crazy angle she was in danger of falling off.

'I decided that from this day forth you could come
out of your hiding place and stay out.' He hauled a
large suitcase from the top of the wardrobe. 'And in
case you're wondering what to wear. . . Chris and Helen
took themselves to Melbourne last weekend and had a
buying spree.'

'I'll kill them. . .'

'Look what they bought you before you kill them.'
And he tipped the contents of the suitcase over the bed.

Annie was effectively silenced. She sat stunned, sur-
rounded by a mound of tissue and ribbon, and her new
husband sat down on the bed and started opening
parcels.

He didn't say a word. Just silently held up one garment after another.

Helen and Chris had started from the skin out.

There were tiny, frothy pieces of lace that Annie
recognized—but only just—as a far-flung relation to
the sensible cotton knickers and bras that she wore.

There were silk slips and sheer, slinky pantihose.

There were nightgowns—two—and Annie blushed
just to look at them. She would never have bought
herself anything like this—not in a million years.

She looked up at Tom—and then looked away
quickly. The toad was having a ball.

He was lifting each garment for inspection and then

solemnly laying it before her—as though she'd really accept them!

There were two dresses—short and summery. Far too short! And skirts that were possibly meant for work, only they were tiny and cut to fit revealingly around her thighs. They'd had her measurements, of course, Annie realized. Chris's mum had made her wedding dress, and Annie had wondered at the time why she'd had to measure *everything*.

It went on. Three blouses—fine silk and soft, embroidered lawn. Tailored pants, and a lovely linen jacket that Annie was almost tempted to reach out and touch.

Almost. Not quite.

'Well, now you've unpacked it you can just pack it all back up again, Tom McIver,' she said in a tone that was dangerously quiet. 'None of this is the sort of thing I wear.'

'That's just it. It should be.' Tom lifted a tiny wisp of lace and held it up in awed admiration. 'Not that you'll get to wear it long. Not now I'm your husband.'

'Tom. . .'

'You don't have a choice, Annie. There's nothing else.' He motioned down to the floor. The mess of bleach and soy sauce had done its job well. 'I agree— you'll need more clothes so in a week or so maybe you and Chris could go back to Melbourne and choose some.'

You and Chris. . .

A quiver of doubt crept into Annie's daze. *You and Chris. . .*

Not *you and I*.

Somehow she made herself concentrate on what was important. 'Tom, I liked my jeans and T-shirts.'

'No.' Tom shook his head, leaned over and took her face between his hands. He kissed her gently on the lips. A feather kiss. A kiss of reassurance. A kiss of friendship.

Again she felt that quiver of doubt.

'If I thought you really liked them I wouldn't have done this,' he told her. 'But you hate your clothes, Annie. You've married me, and my marriage is a gift. I now have a wife and a mother for my child. I tried to figure out what I could give you in return, and this is what I came up with. You're beautiful, Annie, and somewhere in the past someone's taken that image away from you. I'm giving it back. You're beautiful and I'm proud of you, jeans or no jeans. Now, though, in these the rest of the world can see the Annie I'm seeing.'

'Tom. . .'

'Not another word.' Tom straightened as a knock at the door outside sounded over Tiny's and Hoof's frantic scratching. 'I think the family's back.'

He walked over and opened the door, and his family surely was back. With a vengeance!

Tiny and Hoof burst in and flung themselves straight through into the bedroom to their very favourite place— Tom's bed. They landed right in the middle of Annie's lingerie, and by the time Edna Harris carried Hannah into the living room Tiny was turning wild circles around the living room, barking in full voice—and wearing a pair of silky crimson knickers on his head.

Edna stopped dead.

'Well. . .'

But the best was yet to come.

Hoof grabbed a wispy bra between his teeth and headed after Tiny. Annie made a frantic grab at Hoof as he headed out of the bedroom, and missed by a mile. She sprawled onto the carpet. Stark naked.

There was nowhere to hide. Hoof knocked the bedroom door wide open as he charged back through to the living room, and Edna looked straight in at Annie. The good lady's jaw sagged so fast that Tom took Hannah in a hurry in case she dropped her.

'Thanks, Mrs Harris,' Tom said blandly over the barking, and only the faintest tremor in his voice showed he was aware of anything unusual. 'We're grateful to you for looking after Hannah last night, but we'll be right now. We're a family.'

Annie lay on the carpeted floor in her birthday suit among dogs and knickers and chaos, and couldn't figure out whether to laugh or cry.

Her married life had begun.

Maybe her doubts were futile. Maybe it could work.

'You don't need to worry about us,' Tom was saying as he gently propelled Edna out of the door. 'We have all we need.'

But did they?

CHAPTER TEN

AFTER two months of marriage they might have been married for years, but Annie's doubts, rather than fading, just grew.

In a way, her life changed dramatically. She took her courage in both hands and wore the new clothes, and even bought more. They certainly made her feel different.

In other ways, nothing changed at all.

It was as if they'd been married for thirty years, she told herself. Tom treated her as a dear, familiar thing—a partner and friend and, at night, a lover. But only at night. During the day they were two very separate people.

The hospital ran as smoothly as before. Maybe more smoothly because Tom was around more and there were no women to distract him. Certainly Annie didn't distract him. His free time he spent with Hannah, and Annie wasn't invited. Annie had free time when Tom was on call, and when he had free time she was on duty.

It was a strange marriage!

At least they didn't fight, and at night, unless their work called them away, Annie could snuggle into Tom's arms and pretend he really was her husband.

Only he wasn't. In the morning he was back to being friend and colleague, and the pretence faded to bitter reality.

She wasn't his wife in the true sense. She wasn't his love.

It was as if he'd opened his bedroom to her—as if he knew that sex was what marriage was about—but he hadn't figured what else was involved. Or even realized that anything more was required.

Annie didn't have the courage to teach him. She held herself back, fearful of being too pushy. Of making him tired of her. If he found her presence cloying then maybe in time he wouldn't even want her in his bed.

It should have gradually become better, she told herself. That was what she so desperately wanted. But although she was falling more deeply in love with her husband by the minute—and although Hannah and the dopey Tiny and Hoof had become such a part of her life that she knew she could never leave them—Tom still held himself apart. He talked to her about Hannah and he talked about their work, but he didn't talk about what he himself felt.

That one day by the beach when he'd spoken of his childhood had been a rare glimpse inside the man, Annie thought, and she started to fear that a glimpse was all she would ever get.

'Give him time, dear,' Helen told her, seeing a look of pain wash over Annie's face on the anniversary of two months of married life. Annie was gazing out of a hospital window to where Tom had Hannah down by the river. Tom was floating a tiny wooden boat in the shallows, the dogs were racing along to catch it in the current and Hannah was crowing her delight in her father's arms. Annie was so jealous she could weep.

Time . . .

'He just doesn't know what marriage is about.' Helen looked again at Annie's face and sighed. 'He'll learn.'

'Will he?'

'Why don't you go down and join them?' Helen suggested. 'I'll call if I need you.'

Annie shook her head.

'He wouldn't want me.'

'But. . .'

'Oh, he'd act pleased to see me,' Annie said sadly. 'He'd smile a welcome—and then wonder why the hell I came. And next time he still won't think of inviting me. He. . .he still needs his personal space.' She

shrugged and turned away—and Helen watched her
with troubled eyes.

At least there was still work. The work she loved.

She looked along the corridor to where Kylie
Manning was practising walking with her crutches.

'You're going beautifully, Kylie,' she called, and
wandered up to talk to Kylie's mother. Anything was
better than staring out of that damned window.

Kylie had been back at Bannockburn for a week,
having been transferred from the Melbourne hospital
where her knee had been reconstructed. In another few
days she could go home. Once Betty was organized.

'I've just walked out of my past life,' Betty Manning
told Annie, as Kylie proudly navigated the hospital corridors. She fingered the angry scar running from cheek
to temple. 'I can't bear to move back. I guess. . .I guess
I'm too scared of what might happen. I'm moving into
a flat in town.'

'Does he hit you?' Annie asked, and as the colour
washed out of Betty's face she didn't need an answer.

'You know, if you had legal advice you could possibly ask Rod to leave and let you and Kylie stay in the
house,' Annie told her diffidently. The Mannings lived
in a huge house, set on thirty acres of prime grazing
land. They had stables of beautiful horses. Two cars
and five garages to put them in. Swimming pool and
tennis courts. . .

'I don't want it.' Betty's voice was flat. 'It's mort-
gaged to the hilt and I've always been uncomfortable
living somewhere that I owed so much money on. No.'
Betty shook her head, her eyes on her injured daughter.
'Rod can keep his house and his lifestyle. I hope. . .I
guess I hope it'll make him less bitter this way—if I
ask for nothing. A bit more likely to accept what's
happened and not to take his anger out on Kylie.'

'You'll ask for nothing at all?'

'Nothing.' Betty sighed. 'I've taken a few things that
belonged to my mother but otherwise—well, you know

I have a part-time job in the local real estate agent's office. Mr Howith's offered to put me on almost full time. He's lovely. He says I can have school holidays off. He and his wife helped me find the flat, and with their help we'll survive.'

'It's a hell of a change for you, Betty.'

Both Annie and Betty started. Unnoticed, Tom had entered the hospital. He was cradling his daughter in his arms, there was river mud on his shoes and his jeans were wet to the knees—hardly professional at all—but his tone was richly sympathetic and Betty gave him an uncertain smile.

'I know, Dr McIver. But. . .' She shook her head. 'Rod's been frightening me for years. Yes, he's hit me—and he's hit Kylie. It only happens when he's drunk and he's always sorry afterwards, but he's been drunk too often. There's nothing left between us. I used to think that things—material possessions, appearances—were important, but I've finally decided that anything—*anything*—is better than a loveless marriage.'

'Hmm.' Tom cast a curious glance at Annie and then looked away. 'And will Rod have access to Kylie?'

'If he wants it. But he hasn't. . .he hasn't even visited us. Not once. I had to find him when I got out of hospital and tell him what I've decided. It's hard. I don't want Kylie to grow up without a father but. . . If he wants access I'm asking for a court order that he can't drink when he has her.' She hesitated.

'Well, maybe if I'm not around to annoy him he won't drink so much anyway. He's charming to his friends. A real gentleman. So I can only hope.' She gave them a bright smile—a smile of courage.

'Anyway, Kylie and I have something we've been meaning to ask you,' she continued, smiling at Tom. 'Kylie's coming home from hospital—home to our new little flat—next Friday, and the following Saturday it's her birthday. She's six. We thought we'd have a party to celebrate. Not much. Just. . .just a few friends with their children. Bread and butter and hundreds and thousands, little red sausages and red cordial.'

Betty's smile deepened as her daughter finally made it back to her side, and her hand came out to tousle Kylie's bright red curls. 'But Kylie and I would love it if you could bring Hannah. We thought it'd be an honour—a house-warming gift to us—if we could have Hannah at the very first birthday party she's ever attended.'

'I see.' Tom chuckled and stooped to address Kylie. 'Well, Hannah would consider it an honour to attend your sixth birthday party, Miss Manning,' he told her, as his boots squelched river water onto the hospital corridors. Matron Robbie would have a fit! 'I'll bring her myself. What time would you like me to come?'

Me . . .

The word hung in the air, and Betty looked uncertainly at Annie.

'I thought you all. . .' she faltered.

'Annie's on call on Saturday afternoons,' Tom told her.

'But. . .don't you ever go out together?'

'We don't. . .'

'Annie can't. . .'

Their answer was spoken in unison, and Annie found herself staring at the floor. Anywhere but at Tom.

'Saturday's busy,' Tom explained. 'Sports injuries. . .'

'But I have the phone on and it's only two minutes' drive from the flat back to the hospital.' Betty was staring in bewilderment from one to the other. 'Unless. . .unless you don't want to come, Dr Burrows.'

'Of course I'd like to come,' Annie said stiffly. 'Tom's right, though. There are sports injuries on Saturdays. I'll come in my own car in case I'm called away.'

There. She'd go separately. And once there she'd

have a celebratory glass of red cordial and slip away before she cramped Tom's style. He wasn't used to having a wife by his side.

'It'll be better if you all come,' Kylie confided, slipping her small hand into Tom's. 'We've invited my dad and we hope he comes, too.' Her small face puckered. 'I *need* my mum *and* my dad—and I bet your baby does too. She's just not old enough to ask yet.'

My mum and my dad. . . That was what Annie and Tom were supposed to be. A family.

Betty Manning's eyes blinked back tears—and it was as much as Annie could do not to join her.

'Why don't you want me to go with you?'

Annie and Tom were sitting over roster sheets—a task Annie found infinitely depressing. It was getting worse. *You work Saturday, I'll work Sunday. I'm taking Hannah out to Dave McCrae's farm on Wednesday so can you cover me here? If you're going to Lisa Myrne's kitchen tea then I'll work.*

If you'll be here then I'll be there. And vice versa. Portrait of a marriage.

'Go?'

'To Kylie's birthday party,' Annie said bluntly. 'Why don't you want me to go with you, Tom?'

'I do.'

'No.' Annie shook her head. 'You don't. It sticks out of a mile. Even Betty could see it and she thought it really strange. It's like. . .now we're married you're uncomfortable when I'm around. As if you don't know how to treat me.'

'That's not true.'

'I guess it is,' Annie said sadly. 'Tom, the valley is expecting you to treat me as a wife—and you still treat me as a medical colleague.'

'I do treat you as a wife, Annie.' Tom's hand reached out to grasp hers and she pushed herself back from him.

'No.'

'Annie. . .'

'You don't understand, do you, Tom?' she said slowly, and all at once it was unbearable. What he was asking of her. 'You don't understand that I've put myself into an almost impossible situation.'

'OK,' he said, his eyes watchful. 'I *don't* understand. Explain.'

Explain. . . How on earth could she explain?

'I thought. . . Well, I talked myself into believing that this could work.' Annie rose and looked down at him. Looked down at her love. 'I wanted it so much, you see. But I didn't count on how you made me feel. . . how going to bed with you would change things.'

Tom's dark eyes met hers and searched, trying hard to follow what she meant. That was the trouble, Annie thought bitterly. He was so damned kind. So understanding. If there was a right thing to do then Tom McIver would do it.

But he couldn't do the right thing now. How could he understand the role Annie wanted him to fill when that role was so ill-defined that Annie was hard put to explain it to herself.

'When I go to bed with you I give myself to you,' Annie told him in a voice that wasn't quite steady. She hauled her white coat around her as if she were cold. 'And every morning you expect me to take myself back. It's sort of like there's two of me. The night-time Annie—and Dr Annie Burrows, colleague. But I'm one person, Tom. I can't do it any more. It's tearing me in two.'

Tom ran his hand through his hair in a gesture that Annie knew and loved. He used it when he was tired. Or worried.

He was worried now.

'Hell, Annie, I'm trying. Trying to make this marriage work, I mean. I don't know what else you can ask of me. I know it's hard, putting up with me and Hannah and the dogs. . .'

'That's just it, Tom,' Annie said sadly. 'It isn't hard.
But I want more. You don't ask enough. I want to
give more. And if you don't understand what I want to
give. . .'

'You're talking in riddles. . .'

'No.' Annie took a deep breath. Helen had counselled
patience, but Annie had run right out of patience. Run
out of sanity. She couldn't keep going like this.

'I've fallen in love with you, Tom McIver,' she told
him, and the whole world stilled as she said the words.
She'd sworn never to say them, but here she was, breaking all her promises.

He still didn't understand. Tom's face softened
instantly and he stood to take her hands.

'But, Annie. . . That's great. Hell, I love you, too.'
She knew he didn't.

'Tom, I'll bet you have old sweaters you love just
as much as me.'

'That's not—'

'Quite true?' Annie shrugged and deep inside her
heart she turned to ice at what she was doing. 'It is,
you know. You love me because I'm your wife and
you're supposed to love your wife. Well, maybe. . .
maybe I'm dreaming of something out of the pages of
one of Chris's romantic novels, but my ideal of someone
who loves me is someone who welcomes me always.
Sure, lovers can be apart. Married couples can be apart.
But, if they really love each other, when they come
together they fit like two halves of a whole. Whereas
you and I. . .'

'We do.'

'No. We don't. I come into the room and you're
polite and kind and welcoming—but you don't really
relax until I leave again.'

'Annie, we're good together.'

'Only in bed.' Annie shook her head, and even though
she knew what she had to say it was all she could
do to get the words out. 'And I can't. . .I can't keep

sleeping with you. Not now. Not now I've told you.'
She sighed, her heart dull with aching loss. To lose him
at night as well. . .

There was no choice. She was starting to feel that at
night she could be anyone. That he turned off the lights
and loved her body. Loved a woman. . . But not her.

'Tom, you want a wife. Well, you still have one. The
wife you wanted. The wife you married me for. I'm
not asking for a divorce. I'll stay here and we'll keep
the door between our apartments open, and I'll be as
much a mother to Hannah as you'll let me. But. . .but
I won't sleep in your bed, Tom. I won't be half a love.
I don't see how any woman can be.'

'Annie, this is crazy.'

'It is, isn't it?' she said dully. 'I was crazy to believe
it could possibly work. But now. . . All I'm asking is
that you keep to your side of your door at night, as well
as by day, and I'll keep to mine. And we'll go from
there. Please, Tom.'

He stared at her, baffled.

'I don't know what the hell else I can do, Annie.'

'No, you don't,' Annie said sadly. 'And that's just
the trouble.'

It was the hardest decision Annie ever made. It was
even harder sticking to it.

At eleven that night, just after she'd crawled between
the sheets in her own bleak bedroom, Tom came through
to find her. He knocked first, as he always did when
he came to her side of the wall. As if she might have
something to hide—like a lover tucked under the bed.

'Annie, I need you.'

She needed him, too.

But she knew from his voice that it wasn't his love
life Tom was talking about. She sat up in bed, hauling
her trusty sheet after her.

'What for?' Her voice was laced with suspicion and
Tom flicked the light on and sighed.

'Not for your sweet self, Annie.' It was odd how his voice sounded dull and flat. Tired. 'But old Mr Howard needs a catheter.'

Jack Howard. . .

Jack Howard was a nursing-home patient and had been for the whole time Annie had been in Bannockburn. He was in care because of 'confusion', but it was Annie's guess that the confusion was assumed. Certainly he was bad-tempered and irrational, but by all reports he'd been that way his whole life.

Jack lorded it over the nursing-home staff. He seemed to enjoy living here much more than living under his daughter's care. Certainly his confusion escalated every time the hospital board thought of sending him home.

'Why does he need a catheter?'

Annie pushed tousled curls from her face and tried to focus on medicine—on something other than Tom, standing at the edge of her bed. Good grief! It hadn't even been twelve hours since she'd told him she wouldn't sleep with him, and already her body was aching with loss.

'He's got a blockage of some sort. Urine retention. It'll have to investigated, but meanwhile he's yelling in pain, his bladder's full to bursting and he won't let me near him.'

Annie grimaced. Jack, with a real reason to complain. . . Oh, dear!

'So. . .'

'I know it sounds stupid,' Tom said wearily, 'but Helen and I have tried all options. He's convinced we're trying to rape him.' The sides of his mouth quirked into a smile. 'Well, maybe he's not convinced, but he's certainly enjoying telling the world that's what we're doing. What he's saying. . .well, it's just as well you're a married lady.'

Tom's smile faded as he looked down at her. 'He needs intravenous sedation, Annie, before he wakes the whole hospital. Can you do it? I've already turned the intercom on between Hannah and Children's Ward.'

It was an arrangement they'd made that suited them. Children's Ward was always staffed at night now so both Annie and Tom were available if needed.

'Of course.' Annie swung her feet out of bed. And then remembered she'd gone to bed as she'd gone to bed for the last two months—with nothing on at all. Her gorgeous nightgowns had proved totally useless. She hastily retired to her sheet. 'You. . .you go ahead. I'll be there in five minutes.'

'Three,' Tom said harshly, and his face was bleak. 'The pain's bad, and your modesty takes second place.'

It was a tricky procedure. Inserting a catheter was simple in a compliant male, but Jack certainly wasn't compliant. By the time Annie reached the ward he was roaring like a stuck pig and Annie couldn't decide whether it was from pain or indignation.

Mostly indignation, she guessed. Pain made people weak, and there was no weakness behind the old man's protests. The social workers had been in the day before, Annie remembered, trying to talk him into returning home. Therefore, if there was something wrong with him he'd play it up for all it was worth, and if there was a fuss to be made Jack would make it. They hadn't a hope of making him see reason. When Jack saw Annie he reacted with the fury of an active volcano.

'Bloody woman! Get the hell away from me. You leave me private parts alone. And you. . .' He jabbed a finger up at Tom. 'You oughta be ashamed of yourself. Let a man alone.' Then a spasm of pain caught him and he left out a roar of indignation that life could treat him with so little dignity.

If he hadn't been hurting Annie could have almost found it in herself to smile. And if she hadn't been hurting. . . Tom's voice cut across Jack's moans. 'Jack, we're here to stop your pain. Nothing else. Now shut up and let us get on with it.'

'You young b——'

'Jack, shut up or I'll pack you home to your daughter first thing tomorrow.'

Annie blinked at Tom's bluntness, but the bluntness seemed to help. The old man stared up in speechless indignation, and stayed still long enough for Tom to hold him——no mean feat in itself——while Annie quickly administered a sedative. The bluster started again as Jack felt the prick of Annie's needle, but by then it was too late.

The bluster died, allowing Annie to get a word in edgewise.

'Mr Howard, I've given you something to stop the pain and let you sleep. Just relax and let it work.'

The fast-acting drug was already taking hold, and Jack Howard's eyes showed real confusion now.

'I'll make it long-lasting. It's no use settling him if he rouses just as angry as he is now,' Annie told Tom, as Jack slumped back on his pillows. 'He'll haul the catheter straight out again.'

Jack wasn't quite finished.

'Bloody women just want a man's body. Bloody sexpot. . .' And he drifted peacefully into drug-induced sedation. Sexpot! Yeah, right! There was a certain irony in being called a sexpot when she'd just sworn off sex for life.

Think of something else.

'Why has he blocked?' Annie asked, as Tom carefully inserted the catheter into Jack's penis.

'His prostate's enlarged,' Tom told her, concentrating on what he was doing. 'I was hoping it wouldn't cause him problems, but it has now. We'll have to do something about it, but can you imagine doing a prostate operation on Jack?'

'No,' Annie said bluntly. 'Thank God I'm not a urologist.'

'That makes two of us. He'll have to go to Melbourne for the operation, and heaven help the urologist who has to examine him first. There!' Tom stood back from the bed as the urine bag started to fill. 'Whew, see the pressure. That pain wasn't assumed. The poor old coot must have been in agony.' He shook his head. 'We'll transfer him to Melbourne tomorrow and see if we can get him operated on by the weekend.'

'His daughter won't like it.' Annie knew his daughter well. She was forceful, tough, thoroughly unpleasant— and furious that her father didn't show the least sign of dying. She'd tried to have him certified totally incompetent so she could assume control of his farm, but Jack's confusion magically lifted every time he saw a lawyer.

The sooner Jack died and let his daughter get hold of his farm and money the better pleased she'd be, Annie knew. If he went to Melbourne for an operation Jack was likely to demand a single room and every expensive extra he could get. Which meant less money for his daughter later on. She would be furious.

'She's said no medical intervention at all.'

'Yeah, well, she'll have to lump this,' Tom said grimly. 'Jack's not going to die of an enlarged prostate but it'll make his life miserable. If I must, I'll get permission from the public trustee.'

'She'll fight. . .'

'I can fight, too.' Tom looked grimly at Annie as Helen came into the room to keep watch on the old man. Annie gave Helen directions on Jack's care, but Tom didn't speak again until they were out in the corridor.

'I can fight for what has to be fought for,' Tom reiterated, and his voice was flat. 'Annie, I want you to come back to my bed.'

'Why?'

'Because we both want it.' He managed a smile. 'Tiny and Hoof are missing you.'

'It's midnight on the first night,' Annie snapped. She was dangerously close to breaking. 'They can hardly be pining already. And I'll bet you anything they ate their dinner as if nothing at all was wrong.'

'If they stop eating, will you come back?'

'No!'

'What about if I do?'

'Tom!' Annie stopped dead and turned to the man by her side. 'Tom, why? You don't really want me.'

'I do.' He reached out and grasped her hands in a grip that was sure and strong. 'Annie, I love you in my bed.'

It had been the wrong thing to say.

I love you in my bed.

He did, Annie knew. And that was the whole problem!

'I love you in your bed, too, Tom,' she whispered, and her voice was filled with desolation. 'But I love you all the time. All the time, without stopping. And I've finally figured it's all or nothing. So. . .unless you can figure out what that means. . . Unless you want me always you can't have me in your bed. Because it's like taking a piece of me, and by cutting that part out the rest of me can't survive.'

CHAPTER ELEVEN

WHAT followed were bleak and lonely days.

Luckily the hospital was busy. There was little time to sit and mope. In her free time—the time when Tom was neck-deep in work because he'd pencilled in Annie as absent—Annie took the dogs to the beach or carried Hannah down to the river and played with her.

She could leave. She could get a divorce.

But when she held Hannah...when she sat by the river and held her so her tiny feet kicked the water... when she watched her face crease into Tom's delighted smile... Annie knew she could do no such thing.

Tom had invited her to be a part of Hannah's life and now she couldn't walk away from that. She'd fallen head over heels in love with two people—with Tom, and with his little daughter.

Despite the yawning gulf between Annie and Tom, she knew she could still be a mother to this little one. Watch her grow... She couldn't leave Hannah for reasons that were purely selfish.

And, good grief, she even loved the dogs!

The two crazy mutts were swimming in the currents. Now they lunged out of the water past Annie and stopped just long enough to shake the water from their fur and soak her to the skin.

'Ugh... Horrible dogs. I don't love you. I don't!'

It wasn't true. She did love them, and once again it wasn't just because they belonged to Tom.

Annie held Hannah close and put her lips in the baby's soft curls. She didn't know what on earth she was going to do.

But, whatever it was, she couldn't walk away.

* * *

It was Saturday. The day of Kylie's party.

Annie was on call. She spent the morning seeing patients at clinic, was caught up with a gashed leg, followed by a fractured arm, and at two in the afternoon she went to find Tom—only to discover he'd left without her.

'He told me to say he'd meet you there, as he knew you wanted to take your own car,' the nurse on duty told her.

Fine.

Annie had intended to discuss a gift with Tom but there hadn't been the opportunity. She'd chosen a pretty wall frieze covered with cartoon characters, intended as half house-warming gift and half birthday present.

Would Tom think of taking a gift himself? If so, they'd be taking separate gifts.

Surely not? If it happened it'd be the talk of the valley but, then, sharing a gift would never occur to Tom. It would never occur to him because they weren't a couple. They were two separate people, with only love for one baby, two dogs and medicine in common. And nothing else.

The party was well under way when Annie arrived. Betty's new apartment was at the back of a big, free-standing house, and Annie could hear children's shouts and laughter from out on the road. A bunch of balloons tied to the fence told her she was in the right place, and so did a tribe of children who came whooping round the side of the house.

'You've come!'

Kylie's crutches weren't cramping her style at all. Gorgeous in party pink, Kylie was moving nearly as fast as her friends. She grinned happily up at Annie, words tumbling out in excitement.

'Dr Annie, this is my new party dress that Grandma made me. My grandma's my mum's mum and she visited me all the time I was in hospital. While my leg was in tr-traction she sat by my bed every day and

sewed embroidery on the front and talked about the day
I'd wear it. And now it's finished. Do you like it? I think
it's beeyootiful. . . And you're my second-last guest, Dr
Burrows.'

'I love your dress,' Annie said warmly, stooping to
give her a hug. 'And I'm sorry I'm late, but an old lady
hurt her arm and needed me. Who else is late?'

'Daddy.' Kylie led the way to the door, her crutches
leaving neatly patterned holes on the lawn. 'Mummy
says he mightn't come, but I know he will. It's my
birthday.' Her small face puckered. 'And he must *know*
it's my birthday.'

She shoved the door open with her shoulder, and
then, with chameleon emotion, her grin returned.

'Hey, I'm opening my presents now,' she yelled.
'Want to watch?' And the children crowded in around
her, leaving Annie to bring up the rear.

Tom was already there. He was sitting on a bean-bag
on the floor, with Hannah sleeping in her cocoon
nearby. When Annie entered he gave her a transient
smile which Annie thought looked strained, and then
went back to talking to the cluster of adults with Betty.
Annie stopped by the doorway and didn't go further.

The room was crowded. Betty gave her a smile of
welcome across the room, but by now the children mill-
ing around Kylie formed an effective barrier between
Annie and the adults. Wrapping paper was being scattered everywhere. There was no room for Annie to pass.

Well, it didn't matter. She was content to stay where
she was, out of Tom's range.

Kylie opened Annie's gift first. Her eyes brightened
with pleasure when she saw the frieze.

'It's just perfect,' she crowed. 'I can put it in my
new bedroom, can't I, Mummy?' She turned to Annie
with the manners of a well-brought-up child. 'Thank
you, Dr Annie.' And then she turned to give Tom a
wide smile as well. 'And thank you too, Dr Tom. And
Hannah.'

Annie saw Tom's face still as her own heart sank. Annie had been right, then. He hadn't thought of this—that people would assume they'd share a gift.

Never mind. Annie stood and watched as Kylie opened gift after gift, and she thought of Hannah doing the same thing in six years. Would she herself be around to see it? Could she and Tom work out some relationship by then?

Then Kylie lifted another card, and sounded out the message on the card.

'Is this right, Mummy?' She frowned. 'I think it says it's from Dr Tom and Hannah. Didn't they already give me something?'

The room fell silent. Dear heaven. . .

'We're not very used to being married yet.' Annie's voice stammered into the uncomfortable stillness. 'Dr Tom and I bought a gift between us, but Hannah wanted us to give you her own gift. So one gift's from Hannah and one is from her mummy and daddy. We just got the messages on the cards wrong.'

'Oh.'

If it didn't quell the curiosity of the adults, at least Annie's explanation was satisfactory to Kylie. After all, two gifts were infinitely better than one. Kylie ripped off the wrapping—to reveal an identical frieze to the one Annie had given her.

Some moments are best forgotten.

For once in his life even Tom seemed stumped for words. He looked across at Annie and, as the various adults gave each other 'goodness, won't we be able to talk about this later' looks, Tom's face radiated pure mortification. As if he was suddenly seeing something he hadn't even known existed.

'But. . . Hannah didn't buy her present by herself, did she?' Kylie asked Annie, puzzled. 'Didn't she know what her mummy and daddy were buying? Didn't you tell her?'

'We'll change it for something else, Kylie,' Annie

said gently, her eyes on Tom. And some of the gentleness in her voice was for him. He hadn't known. Whatever family life he'd had in the past hadn't geared him for this. Hadn't geared him for her.

Blessedly, the door swung open just at that moment, and attention was diverted to Kylie's last guest.

'Daddy!' The identical gifts forgotten, Kylie hauled herself to her feet and reached her father without the use of crutches. 'Daddy, you came to my birthday!'

'Yeah, kitten, of course I came. Wouldn't miss it for quids.'

Rod Manning's voice was coarse and slurred with drink, and Annie winced. The man was dead drunk. It was obvious in the way he moved. He stood in the doorway and his body swayed. He tossed an unwrapped box down to the floor and then held onto the doorknob for support.

This was a Rod Manning Annie hardly recognized. He was unkempt and unshaven. His clothes looked as if they'd been slept in, and he couldn't have seen a bath for a week.

Kylie backed away uncertainly.

'Aren't you going to open my present?' Rod laughed and stared aggressively across at his wife, then back to Kylie. 'You open it now. I'll bet your mother hasn't spent as much on you as I have, sweetheart. I'll bet. . .'

Kylie gave him a scared glance and opened her parcel. It was a dress box and inside lay a frock—a fabulous frothy confection of tulle and lace. It looked over-the-top expensive, gaudy, and at least a couple of sizes too small.

'Thank you very much, Daddy,' Kylie whispered, her eyes scared. 'Grandma made me my dress for this birthday but this. . .this can be my next birthday dress. Or. . .' Her voice faltered. 'My Christmas dress.'

'You'll wear *my* dress for your birthday,' Rod growled. 'What do you mean, *'Grandma made me. . .'?* His voice was a cruel mimicry of Kylie's. 'My girl doesn't wear home-made dresses. Go and get changed.'

'But Grandma sewed me my dress while I was hospital.' There was a touch of defiance in Kylie's voice. She stood tall and faced her father square on. Rod Manning might be autocratic, but Kylie was her father's daughter. Rod wasn't having a bar of it.

'Kylie, you heard me. Change!'

'I won't.'

'You little. . .' Rod took a step forward and gave his daughter a ringing slap across the face.

'*No!*' Annie was the closest adult—the only one on Rod's side of the room. As Rod raised his hand again she dived straight at him. She caught his arm in mid-swing and held on like a terrier. 'No, Rod. . .'

'*Don't!*' Tom roared the command almost in unison with Annie's plea. He launched himself like lightning from the other side of the room, but he wasn't fast enough. He wasn't expecting what happened next.

No one was.

Annie was still clinging limpet-like to one of Rod's arms, but with his free hand Rod hauled a gun from the inside pocket of his jacket. And pointed it straight at Tom.

'Get back. Get back and leave my daughter to me.'

Tom stopped dead in mid-stride, wicked blue metal pointing straight at his heart.

'And you. . . Get away, bitch!' Rod pushed Annie away from him with a savage shove before he grabbed his daughter and hauled her close to him.

'She's wearing *my* dress and she's coming home with *me*,' he snarled. 'That's why I brought this.' He waved the gun. 'In case anyone here was stupid enough to object. You think I'd leave her in a dump like this? My kid? My kid doesn't wear home-made clothes and she doesn't live in any dumpy apartment.' He glared across the room at Betty, and his bloodshot eyes were crazy.

'And she doesn't live with you either, slut,' he snarled at his wife. 'Not now. Not ever. I've been to the

lawyer's and they say I won't get custody of her. I
can apply for access, they say. *Access!* Every bloody
weekend and I have to stay off the booze to get her.
You stupid bitch! Do you think I'll let you get away
with that?'

He raised the gun higher over the heads of the children, pointed it straight at Betty—and his finger
tightened on the trigger.

Whether or not he meant to shoot, Annie would never
know. She couldn't wait to find out. He'd shoved her
to the floor. Now she rose like one possessed and lunged
over Kylie's head, hauling the gun sideways from the
child and down—hauling with the determination of
desperate terror.

'*Annie, no. . .*' Tom's roar came from across the room
and he was moving again, but there were terrified children and gifts and furniture crowded between them. He
couldn't reach her in time to help. Annie clung for dear
life—and then the gun exploded.

One single explosion. Nothing more.

After the explosion—silence.

Annie fell silently, crumpling to the floor as her leg
gave way under her.

'*Annie. . .!*'

The gun rose again, and this time it pointed straight
at Kylie, still in Rod's grasp.

'Nobody move. No one!'

Tom froze. He had no choice.

Still gripping Kylie, Rod backed further from the
group of horrified children, and stared down at what
he'd done.

At Annie.

He looked only for a moment. Just long enough to
see a circle of scarlet form and spread on the soft pastel
skirt hugging Annie's thigh.

Then the gun moved away from Kylie and was lev-
elled at Annie again—straight at her heart.

'*No!*'

There were still children between Tom and Rod. Between Tom and Annie. Tom couldn't reach her. His voice was hoarse with fear, but it wasn't fear for himself. It was fear for Annie. 'Manning, don't do it. No.'

'Get back, then.'

Rod grabbed his daughter tighter, and waved the gun around the room. 'Get back, all of you. In fact, you can all get outside. I don't want you here. Go. Now. Move! Leave me with my daughter.'

Tom took another step towards Annie.

'Go now! Or I'll shoot the bitch again! She stays here, too.' The gun swung back to Annie. She was huddled on the floor and the pool of crimson on her thigh was spreading down to soak the carpet. 'I mean it. It's good that I shot her. Good! She's the one that caused the trouble. Gave that sample to the cops. Made me lose my job. My family. It'll give me great pleasure to shoot her again—or let her bleed to death. *Just get!*'

'Manning, you don't mean this. Think of the trouble you're making for yourself if you make this any worse. Rod, don't. . .'

Tom's voice was an urgent plea. Around him, the birthday guests were reacting to terror in different ways. Most of the children were scrambling to reach adults at the far side of the room. One little girl stood stock-still and stared, white with shock, and a toddler picked up Kylie's birthday dress and tipped it out of the box onto his head.

And crowed with delight.

'Get them out! Now!' Rod was speaking directly to Tom—but his gun was on Annie.

'Mannning, she'll die. She's bleeding. . .' There was no mistaking Tom's fear. He gazed down at Annie with desperation and took another step towards her. 'Let me take Annie at least. . .'

'Move one step closer and she'll die a hell of a lot faster. And then the kids. See how many I can kill before someone stops me. I mean it. You clear this room right now—or she gets it. *Move!*'

There was nothing for Tom to do but obey. With one last, despairing glance at his wife, Tom turned to the door at the back of the room.

'All right,' he said heavily—dully. 'Everyone out. Move quietly and quickly.' He picked up Hannah's baby capsule.

Then he turned back.

'If you let her die, there won't be anywhere on God's earth you can hide,' he told Rod Manning, and then he took Betty's hand. The woman seemed stunned to immobility. 'Come on, Betty. We have to leave.'

'Kylie. . .' Betty's voice was a frantic moan. 'He'll kill Kylie.'

'No, he won't,' Tom said harshly, and gave her a push out of the door. 'Not if he has one brain left in his head. He won't do anything so stupid!'

The door swung shut. Inside the room there was silence.

From the other side of the door Annie could hear Betty's voice raised in frantic protest and Tom telling her to hush—to move the children quickly away from the building.

A child was sobbing.

Then there was nothing but Rod's heavy breathing.

Kylie hadn't said a word. She stood absolutely still in Rod's grasp, as if she were beyond protest.

There was blood oozing rapidly from Annie's leg. The bullet had sliced the inside of her left thigh. Annie looked down with detached interest and decided that, professionally, she should do something about it. She grabbed the first thing to hand—Rod's ridiculous party dress—wedged it between her thighs and clenched her legs together. Pressure should stop the bleeding. . . It didn't help much. The blood still came, but she couldn't think what else to do.

Somehow it didn't seem to matter what she did. The

whole room looked surrealistic. There were fairy cakes and sandwiches scattered over the floor, knocked there by one of the terrified children. A cake with pink icing lay by her hand, and there was a smatter of blood on its side.

'You've hurt Dr Annie. She's bleeding.' The voice was Kylie's—matter-of-fact and accusing.

'She deserved it.' Rod's slurred growl.

'No, she didn't, Daddy.'

'Shut up.'

'You shouldn't have shot her.'

'Hush, Kylie.' Annie made a huge effort to make her voice work, and somehow she got the words out. This was important. 'Leave Daddy be.'

'You shut your mouth.'

'What. . .what will you do now?' Annie asked. Her voice came from such a long way away. How much blood had she lost? Too much, she knew. She was feeling dizzy and sick.

'I'll wait, that's what I'll do.' Rod walked to the doors leading out of the room and shoved a bolt home on each. Then he turned to the window. The moment he let Kylie go the child dived to where Annie lay. She put her arms round Annie and huddled close. Annie tried to put an arm around her in return, but her arm seemed far too heavy.

How much blood was she losing? Dear heaven. . .

'Wait. . .wait for what?' she whispered.

'God knows. You to die?' Rod turned to watch her. 'I'd enjoy that.'

'Then you'd be up for murder.'

'Doesn't matter,' he said heavily. 'Lost my job. Without a licence, no job. Bank's foreclosing on the house. No bloody house. No wife. No kid.'

'You do have a child.' It was so hard to make herself speak.

'Look at her,' he sneered. 'What sort of a kid is that for a father to have? Wearing her bloody grandmother's dresses. Living with her mother. Doesn't even want to come near me.'

'Not when you frighten her,' Annie managed. 'And you don't have to frighten her.' She hesitated. 'Please. . . Let Kylie go outside,' she pleaded. 'Don't scare her any more.'

'The kid stays here. 'Till the end.'

Annie looked up into his face—and she knew what he intended. This man was suicidal. Drunk and suicidal. He pulled a bottle from a jacket pocket and took a long swallow of whisky—and then another—and Annie knew. He didn't have the courage to take his own life, but he wanted to be dead.

And he wanted Annie and Kylie to go with him.

After that the world started to drift. There were the sounds of sirens from a long way off.

Kylie was holding her hand and saying, 'Don't go to sleep. Please, Dr Annie, don't go to sleep. I don't want you to go to sleep.' It was so hard to keep her eyes open.

Annie tried desperately to hold Kylie close—to keep her safe—and promise that she wouldn't sleep. But she wasn't able to find the words she needed.

The pain in her thigh was fierce and throbbing.

Still there was silence. It went on and on. The room smelled of whisky and stale beer and, ridiculously, of the cocktail frankfurters congealing on the table.

Rod stood at the window, staring out at the backyard and willing anyone to come into range of his gun.

Kylie huddled closer to Annie, silently weeping.

Mustn't sleep. Mustn't. She had no choice. Annie's lids drifted lower—and suddenly jerked up.

There was a crash of breaking glass, a dull thud and then a vast and terrible smell. A smell that filled the room with fog, and burned and made Kylie choke. . .

But before the child could manage her first cough the silence turned to massive noise. Annie heard the splintering of wood and glass, crashing and shouts, and then a strong male body hurled itself from the stinking fog and covered both her and Kylie with his body.

There was a savage oath from above.

'Don't be a fool!'

A single shot rang out—and a scream.

Then Annie was being lifted and carried out through the fog—out through the burning mist. Somehow she and Kylie were being carried together and she wasn't sure whether one man was carrying her or two—but there was no way she was letting go of Kylie. No way at all.

Who was carrying her? Who? What was happening? Her head wasn't working. She was drifting towards unconciousness but there was one last thing she had to say. She must!

'You mustn't shoot her. I won't—'

'No one will shoot Kylie. Or you. You're safe, my love. You're safe.'

It was Tom. No matter how far away the world was, she'd know that voice anywhere. Her Tom.

She could let go now. Tom was here. She was safe, and he wouldn't let the world hurt Kylie.

And she knew nothing more for a very long time.

CHAPTER TWELVE

SHE shouldn't be in hospital.

Annie woke and stared up at the ceiling in concern. She was in the wrong place. In a ward. She had no business here. She should be standing over the bed, stethoscope in hand and ready to work. Not *in* the bed!

She lifted her head in bewilderment and pushed herself up, only to find strong hands holding her shoulders and pressing her back.

'And where do you think you're going?'

Tom!

'It's OK,' Tom said swiftly, seeing her confusion and flooding fear. 'It's fine, Annie. You're not to be upset. No one's hurt, except you.'

'Kylie. . .'

'Kylie's at home with her mum and her grandma and grandpa. The police have Rod in custody. He tried to turn the gun on himself, but failed.'

'But. . . Tom, I heard. . .I heard a shot. He didn't hurt you?'

'He fired once and missed. And once I stopped coughing I was fine. We used tear gas to get in. The police gave me a mask, but I couldn't see you fast enough so I hauled it off. Yeah, Rod shot at us—but he was blinded and panicking and he missed us by a country mile.'

'And. . .he's really OK?'

'He's really OK.' Tom lifted her hand and held it tightly between his. 'Stop worrying about everyone else, Annie. Think about you.'

'There's nothing. . .'

'Nothing wrong?' Tom closed his eyes, and there

were the shadows of haunting fear still on his face. 'Oh, God, Annie, if you knew how close. . .'

And then, as if he could bear it no longer, Tom gathered her into his arms. He held her, tubes and all. Plasma was being fed into her arm though an intravenous line. There was another line with what must be saline. . . She was strung up like a fish on a multitude of hooks and could go nowhere.

She didn't want to. Tom was holding her as if he'd never let her go, and that was just where she wanted to be.

'Annie. . .'

'Tom. . .what. . .?'

'No, hush and let me speak.' Tom's voice was a low growl, muffled by her hair. 'You've scared me half to death and you owe it to me to let me say what I must. I thought I'd lost the chance for ever.'

'You almost bled to death.' His arms tightened convulsively. 'Thank God the bullet didn't hit an artery. There's only soft tissue damage. The bullet's still in there but it can stay. We'll send you to Melbourne when your electrolytes are up a bit. Get a decent surgeon to remove the bullet and repair the damage. But, oh, Annie. . . You've still got a leg—and a life—but I've lost years from mine. Annie, love. . .'

There was raw agony in Tom's voice and Annie left herself drift, wonderingly, in his hold. There was nothing at all wrong with her when he held her like this. Nothing at all.

But Tom's voice was still filled with pain.

'God, Annie, when we had to go in. . . The police wanted to wait and try to talk him out. . .but I knew you were bleeding to death. We had to risk the tear gas.'

'Annie, I died a million deaths outside while they stuffed around with masks and cannisters and bullet-proof vests. All the time not knowing.' The agony in Tom's voice was turning to anger, but the anger wasn't directed at Annie. It was directed straight at himself.

'I've been such a fool. I thought. . .I thought if you died, you'd die not knowing. . .'

'Not knowing?' Annie's voice was a thread-like whisper, but it drifted out over the room. Filling it with hope.

Waiting. Waiting for a miracle. And the miracle came.

'Knowing that I love you. Knowing that I care for you so deeply. . .and knowing that I was too much of a coward to tell you.'

'Tom. . .'

'I was so damned scared of relationships,' Tom murmured, and his arms held her as if she were the most precious thing in the world. 'Of getting involved. And when I finally figured out just what you were. . .just what I felt for you. . .well, it scared me silly.'

He sighed and buried his face in her hair.

'So I thought I could sleep with you but hold our lives separate. That way. . .well, if you left—*when* you left—it wouldn't be so bad.' He gave a harsh laugh. 'I guess that's a legacy from my past. I loved my parents and they left. I loved my grandmother and she died. So I guess. . .subconsciously I was afraid to let myself love you. Afraid to love anyone. But I had no choice with Hannah. And today. . .from today I don't have a choice with you.'

'Tom, you don't have to. . .'

'Don't have to love you?' Tom's voice was almost a groan. 'You're kidding. Annie, you made the leap in love and trust. On our wedding night you offered me everything, and I shoved you away. I knew, you see. Even before you said you loved me, I knew. I could see it in your eyes. And, like a fool, I thought I could use that love—but not return it.'

He sighed and gently lowered her back on her pillows, then bent to stroke her hair.

He must have given her pethidine, Annie thought

drowsily. She was floating in a mist of love and light and wonder.

'I was a damned fool,' he said bitterly. 'I saw it at the birthday party with the gifts. . . Everyone's faces. . . Everyone seeing that we didn't have a proper marriage. I saw clearly then that the way I was treating you was wrong. But even then. . . While Kylie opened her presents I sat like a fool, trying to figure out whether I wanted to take it any further. Whether I wanted a real marriage, after all. And then some crazy lunatic with a gun comes blasting in and—' He stopped, his voice choking.

His hands moved to grip Annie's shoulders so that he could look clearly into her eyes. 'I've never been so terrified in my life,' he told her.

'Tom. . .'

He put his finger to her lips, silencing her.

'All my life I've held myself apart so that if I lost you. . .if I lost anyone. . .I could keep on being me. Independent Tom McIver.' He gave a bitter laugh.

'Only when Hannah arrived it shook my foundations. I could no longer exist being just me. I saw that. I couldn't bear Hannah being in the world and me not there. And today. . . Today I saw what it would be like. . .if I was in the world and my Annie wasn't.'

He held her hard, his hands gripping her with urgency and his eyes searching hers, while she looked wonderingly up at him.

And then he gave a rueful smile.

'Hell, sweetheart you're exhausted,' he told her. 'You've lost so much blood. You should be sleeping. But I couldn't let another moment go by without telling you. . .that I love you, Annie. I love you with my heart and my soul. I love you with everything I have. And if I lost you. . .if I lost you as I thought today I'd lost you. . .then a part of me I'm only just beginning to realize exists would wither and die. And anything's

better than that. Annie, I never want to be apart from
you again.'

'Tom, do you mean. . .?' Annie was weary and weak
and confused, but she wasn't so confused she couldn't
focus on what he was saying. Not so much on his words,
but on what his eyes were telling her. Tom's eyes were
sending a message all their own. A message of absolute
commitment. A marriage vow all of their own.

'You mean you want to break down the wall between
our apartments?' she whispered.

'Break down the wall?' Tom pulled her tenderly back
into his arms, mindful of tubes and attachments. 'Hell,
just hand me a sledgehammer. Annie, if there's so much
as ten feet between us from now on it's too much. I'll
never let you go again. If you'll have me, Annie. . . If
you still want me. . .'

'Oh, Tom. . .' Annie's face nestled against Tom's
chest. There was no pain. There was no terror or despair.
There was only joy.

'I thought I was Sunday's bride,' she whispered into
the place above his chest where his heart beat just for
her. 'I thought I was lucky you married me before
waiting for Monday's edition. But, Tom. . . Oh, Tom,
Sundays last for ever.'

Jean Herrington stared out through the palm trees at the
couple on the beach. She ought to go and clean out the
third unit, she told herself. There was another honeymoon couple due in this afternoon.

But she didn't move. For the moment, Jean was content to stay where she was and watch one happy ending.

The Herringtons took only three couples at a time at
their exclusive honeymoon resort. Emerald Palms was
tucked into tropical rain forest on the coast of far north
Queensland. Secluded gardens drifted down to the
beach, and islands off the coast dotted the bay like
jewels set in the glittering sea.

Emerald Palms was a honeymoon resort to dream of for ever.

Jean paid attention to detail, she did, and everything was just right. She should bustle on—but the group on the beach held her in thrall.

'I dunno, Bill,' she told her husband. 'I'm having trouble coping with who belongs where with this lot. Two honeymoon suites for one couple. . .'

'Yeah, but it's not just a couple.' Bill grinned. 'It's a honeymoon with a difference. A man and woman, a baby and a babysitter and two ruddy great dogs. . .' He shook his head and smiled benignly at his wife. 'I know you said we oughtn't take the dogs, but that fella could talk the Pope into turning Methodist!'

'*Bill*!' Jean gave a reluctant grin and conceded. 'I know what you mean, though. He is. . .persuasive. And, oh, Bill, they seem so happy.'

'Just perfect.' Bill came up behind his wife and gave her a squeeze around her ample waist. 'They're what we had in mind when we set this place up. I've never seen a pair so in love. Apart from us, of course.'

Jean wriggled happily in his grasp.

'You can tell the couples that'll last.' She sighed happily. 'And they will. They can't keep their eyes off each other. Or their hands.' Then she giggled at what her husband's hands were doing. 'Get away with you. We're too old to be engaging in hanky-panky at eleven in the morning.'

'We're not too old.' Bill looked out to where Tom was carrying his bride down to the surf. 'Do you reckon they'll ever be too old?'

'Maybe not.' Jean gave her husband a fond kiss and turned her eyes to the couple now knee-deep in the surf. 'I guess not.'

There was no doubt at all that they'd never be too old. Not in Tom's heart. Not in Annie's. Not in the minds of anyone who knew them.

'I hate the idea of this ending,' Annie whispered. She lay contentedly in the arms of her love and looked out over at the distant islands. 'We've only explored three islands and I can count at least five more. And we're going home tomorrow.'

'I have news for you,' her love informed her, kissing her tenderly on the lips. 'Ugh, you taste of salt.'

'Don't you want me, then?' Annie pouted, teasing, and Tom's eyes flared. There was no mistaking the message behind them.

He made a change of direction. He had been carrying her into the surf for a swim.

'*No*!' Annie protested as he turned to carry her up the beach to the honeymoon suite beyond the palms.

She shouldn't have teased him. What a thing to say! Red rag to a bull! It was far too close from here to the bedroom—and she'd wanted a swim.

Past tense.

Well, maybe a fast swim. And then. . .

'What news do you have?' she begged. 'Tell me, Tom, and stop thinking what you're thinking immediately.'

'Aren't you thinking what I'm thinking, too?'

She blushed. Annie's whole body started heating up, from the toes up. 'I might be,' she admitted. 'But tell me first. What news?'

'Just that the locum we employed so we could come away has agreed to take up a permanent position,' Tom told her, and his grip tightened on her near-naked body. 'So we can extend our honeymoon, and when we return we can keep the honeymoon going. When we're off duty, Annie, love, we're off duty together. We're a pair. Inseparable. Bonnie and Clyde. . . Darby and Joan. . .'

'Abbott and Costello?' Annie chuckled contendedly and wound her arms around the neck of her love. 'Ren and Stimpy? Oh, Tom. . . Oh, my Tom. . .'

'So now we have all the time in the world.' Tom sighed in utter contentment and nuzzled his face against her hair. Then he took a deep breath and, before she could utter any more protests, started striding swiftly up the beach with his bride held tightly in his arms.

'So. . .so why are you in such a hurry, then?' Annie said breathlessly, laughing. The heat in her body was escalating to white-hot. Her swim was forgotten. 'If there's all the time in the world.'

'Because I'm starting to think it's not long enough,' her love told her, and the passion in his voice was an aching need. 'Not long enough to even begin to share my love.'

'For ever won't be long enough for all the love in my heart.'

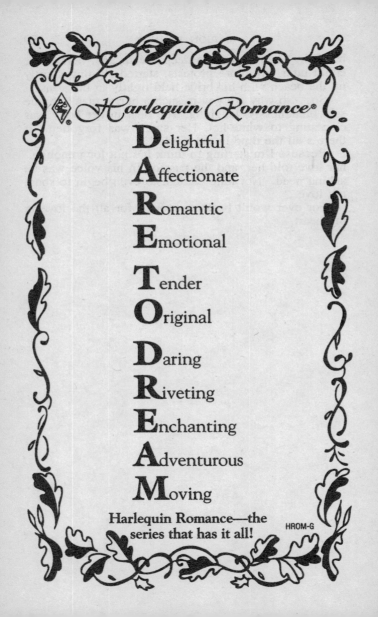

Harlequin Romance®

Delightful

Affectionate

Romantic

Emotional

Tender

Original

Daring

Riveting

Enchanting

Adventurous

Moving

Harlequin Romance—the
series that has it all!

HROM-G